Into the Ruins

Summer 2019

Issue 13

COPYRIGHT

Published July 2019 by Figuration Press
Portland, Oregon

Into the Ruins is a project and publication of Figuration Press,
a small publication house focused on alternate visions of the future
and alternate ways of understanding the world,
particularly in ecological contexts.

intotheruins.com

figurationpress.com

ISBN 13: 978-1-950213-00-9
ISBN 10: 1-950213-00-5

Editor's Note:
Persevering in the face of technological failure.
Just another day of industrial decline.

Comments and feedback always welcome at editor@intotheruins.com
Comments for authors will be forwarded.

Issue 13
Summer 2019

TABLE OF CONTENTS

PREAMBLE

STORIES

CODA

PREAMBLE

IN PARTNERSHIP

BY JOEL CARIS

ONE OF MY GARDEN BEDS IS A RIOT OF FLOWERS.

I can only take the smallest amount of credit for it. They came on their own, seeded last year by me but a result of self-seeding this year. The box is bursting with vining nasturtiums, vigorous calendula, and sprawling borage. It is brilliant in color and chaotic in design. Within this outpouring of petal and leaf are a few tomato plants, a zucchini plant, some beans and chives. It is more the type of design you might expect to find in a garden box as opposed to what I am used to growing: beds, rows, straight lines, vegetables, food. I come, after all, from farming. My tendency is to focus on food first and foremost, with any concerns of beauty (at least, in the traditional sense) secondary.

That is, until my wife Kate wanted flowers. It was far from a request I found outrageous; despite my aforementioned affinity for growing food above all else, I love to see farms and gardens enhanced with the beauty of a good array of flowers. I also take a distinct pleasure in variety and abundance, in a growing space maximized and well used. Seeing vegetable plants nestled among flowers and cozied up against herbs is a particular kind of pleasure I will never turn down, and admittedly far more satisfying a sight to me than just straight rows of vegetables. So the request for flowers was one I not only was happy to fulfill but that I appreciated. In an effort to fulfill it last year, I scattered an edible flower mix across a section of the garden box that this year is so laden with flowers while also planting sunflowers along the edge of a few other garden beds abutting our fence line. While the sunflowers struggled, edible flowers grew and blossomed with vigor, necessitating their occasional knocking back to keep the vegetables they grew alongside from being suffocated. I allowed the flowers to run their course, ripening to seed and planting themselves for this year, for the self-perpetuation now so brightly in bloom.

Near the aforementioned garden bed is a double line of pots holding down the east side of our back patio. These are Kate's work, along with plenty else in our front and back yards. Blazing star, nasturtium, rosemary, poppies, thyme, chocolate cosmos, lavender and more emerge from these pots, adding yet another element to the variety and beauty of our summertime array. My wife tends them closely, watering with captured greywater from our showers, trimming and deadheading the plants as needed, and replanting the pots when necessary. Her attention radiates outward from there, into the raspberries and black caps, the blueberries and roses, the ornamental shrubs and bushes strewn throughout the yard. The last few years I have given her a sturdy pair of Felcos and a well made trowel as gifts; she has made good use of the both of them. It makes me happy.

The yard and garden, in other words, is a team effort. We split the work and the planning and she helps keep me from losing sight of the flowers while I zero in on bringing food to the table. But the flowers, of course, are also food. They are food for bees, pollinators, insects—so many tiny creatures, many of which I do not even recognize. While the beauty of the flowers makes me happy, I think it is the sight of insects on them that brings me the most joy. There is little I enjoy more than going out into the garden on a lovely spring or summer day and finding a large contingent of tiny pollinators flitting and buzzing around on the nasturtiums and borage and calendula and lavender, finding their food in amongst ours, the garden a shared meal.

This is also one of the reasons I so often leave brassicas (kale, broccoli, mustards, and so on) to bolt and flower. One of the reasons is that they still are productive right up to the point of, and even beyond, their flowering. Kale, for instance, continues to put off leaves worth eating even as they start to bolt and by the time they get far enough into the process that the leaves are not worth the effort, the bolting turns them into prolific providers of kale raab. Similarly, many varieties of broccoli will put off side shoots after the main head has been cut, often times for weeks or longer, thus extending the harvest long beyond the main event. Tend to a well established brassica long enough and a single plant can give you a surprising amount of food over the course of weeks or even months. And when I finally do let them go and leave them to flower and seed? Well, the food continues—just not for me, but for insects instead.

The yellow flowers of a bolting brassica are, so far as I can tell, manna to a large number of local pollinators. I have found plenty of honey bees and bumblebees on them before, but more fascinating to me is the impressive variety of unidentified pollinators for which I have no name: so many other tiny bees and flies that do not fall into the most familiar of categories and of which I have yet to take the time to learn to identify. Many of these are small enough that I do not immediately see them until I take a closer look, at which point a larger and busier world of feeding and pollination becomes evident. Rather than the ruggedness of the most familiar bees, often these insects are not just small but slim, elongated, or otherwise sleek and fragile in appearance. Plenty of times in recent years I have found myself standing in my garden near some flowering brassica or another, peering close at the tiny critters flitting here and there amongst the blossoms, their tiny bodies quivering as they eat. It is a particular kind of satisfaction, one of the primary ones for me when it comes to gardening.

Unfortunately, our yard is not fully ours, as we live in a four-plex with gardeners on retainers. Also unfortunately, they have a tendency to whack and hack and sometimes even spray the yard into submission—I suspect to give them as much time as possible before they have to return—and often in the process undo some recent careful tending of Kate's. It is one of the reasons we imagine a day in which we own our own house and have full control over our own yard. Kate is insistent that we will not have grass, or only have the most minimal of patches; the yard is to be for flowers and food and plants alone, and the intent is for it to be a sanctuary for birds and insects. It is not uncommon for us, as we walk around the city, to see some lovely yard brimming with native plants and garden beds identified as Pollinator Habitat with a sign from the Xerces Society or Certified Backyard Habitat with a sign from the Audubon Society and Columbia Land Trust. These serve as inspiration to us, both to do what we can today within our constraints to support pollinator, bird, and other wildlife habitat and to aspire to something more in a future in which we may have more control over a small piece of land in Portland or elsewhere.

It's a small ethos, but one in which I very much believe. While we do not have full control over our yard, we have been able to negotiate with our landlord for partial control. In the backyard, for instance, sits an old and broken down chicken coop, along with a small fenced off area in which the chickens used to roam. It has not seen poultry in years, though. When we first moved in, I imagined fixing up the coop and acquiring a few chickens, bringing with me into the city a small mark of the rural life I was at that time leaving behind. But the logistics of keeping the birds alive and safe from raccoons, possums, coyotes and other predators despite my semi-regular multi-day trips out to the coast and my wife's arrival home from work after dark during the shorter days of the year proved more than I felt willing to tackle.

After a year of this bit of backyard infrastructure remaining unused, and after watching the hired gardeners give the fenced off area next to the coop a good dousing of glyphosate to keep the weeds down, I decided to hazard a reclamation project of the abused bit of land. With our landlord's permission, I proceeded to clear out the weeds the next year and put in some new garden beds. This proved a bit more work than I planned as I discovered that the entire area was covered with a weed cloth about an inch down into the soil, So I had to dig down into that, rip out the cloth, and then break apart and turn the compacted soil beneath, which showed little signs of life.

The result over the past two years is not perfection, but it does include several new garden beds in which I have grown shelling peas, tomatoes, rhubarb, cucumbers, zucchini, green beans, sunflowers, kale, and basil. Presumably (hopefully) the glyphosate has long dissipated. Given the vigor of the plants I have grown in the space, it seems also that some of the nutrients from the previous chicken tenants so many years ago must remain. Or perhaps the long-abused soil beneath the weed mat was simply waiting for its moment to shine. Aside from the vigorous growth of what I have planted and tended in the space, I've noticed an increase in earthworms each year as I've worked the soil. It seems that my efforts to reclaim this small bit of land and bring it at least somewhat into better health have succeeded.

To be honest, this small accomplishment is one of my more satisfying ones. Playing even a small role in fostering new life or in restoring and improving some small portion of my surrounding ecosystem is, to my mind, one of the greater tasks at hand. That I can help feed my wife and myself in the process is just an added bonus, a gift from the larger systems and processes of life surrounding us.

A few years back, I purchased *Farming with Native Beneficial Insects* at the Oregon Small Farms Conference, which takes place in Corvallis at Oregon State University every February. It is a Xerces Society Guide, a book in service of better farming, offering insights on how to bring beneficial insects onto the farm to benefit the growing of food and increase the health of our native insect populations. It talks of cover crops, hedge rows, field borders, insectary strips, insect habitat, and so much more. I bought it with the idea that I might yet find myself returning to farming, and one of my long-held goals for any future farming I might do—farming or even large-scale gardening over which I held control—would be to better integrate beneficial insects and bird and pollinator habitat into my use of the land. I wanted to farm in partnership with these tiny creatures.

While life has a way of surprising, at this point I do not expect to return to farming in any sort of ownership capacity. The book, therefore, is likely of limited value to me. And yet, glancing through its pages, I still feel a yearning to accomplish the goals set out within. Plenty of the information found in the book is usable on a smaller scale, and I imagine ways in which I may put its strategies to work even on a city lot, even in the bustle of an urban area such as Portland.

Even though I still relish the idea of what I might do with an actual plot of land —nothing huge, even just an acre or less—I more and more realize that my efforts are important at all scales. Indeed, I may be more likely to succeed in my imagined partnership at the scale of a yard than that of a farm; I do, I must admit, have a tendency to dream big and then struggle in the implementation of those dreams. More importantly, the concept that anything of benefit must be done at a grand scale is one that I continually reject in theory and just as often in practice. This world is closing in on eight billion strong in population and it is going to take the individual and modest efforts of all of us to bring this planet back into balance if we want to have agency in that process as a species. A few billion global citizens tending tiny pieces of land in ways that enhance biodiversity, bring life to soil, create food for humans and non-humans alike, conserve nutrients, and ensure the health of those creatures that live upon that piece of land is the kind of restoration and mitigation we need. It will only be done if enough people care to do it.

This is always the belief and understanding I come back to. The way we move forward and help undo the destruction that we have caused on this planet—to communities both human and non-human alike—is to come to the world around us with care and affection, with the desire to do better and to foster, support, and create new life in all its forms. It is to seek out some small place—a piece of land, a relationship, a community organization, a nearby stream, something small and intimate and graspable, with which it is natural to form a relationship—and to figure out how to make that place better. It is to see the mason bee, the ladybug, the bumblebee, the green lacewing, or the hoverfly—and then to want to see more of them, to be willing to do whatever it takes to see more of them. It is to look upon a garden box bursting with flowers and herbs and vegetables at the height of summer, during those very long days of sun, and to take heart in the abundance it represents and the ways in which all these different kinds of life take root and grow and flower and sprawl their way across this lovely, inspiriting world of ours. It is to feel summer's warmth, to be happy to be alive, and to want to be surrounded by so many other living things, by all the creatures we share this world with—and to be willing to give some small part of ourselves to make that happen.

Early in the spring, coming out of winter when it is still cold and wet and so much of the world is hunkered down within itself, I begin to think about and imagine the garden and plan where and what to plant. The garden beds—in the yard, in the chicken coop—are mostly blank slates at that point, expanses of soil waiting to be brought to life. And in the early days, when those first seeds and starts go into the soil and those first two leaves, the cotelydons, emerge out tiny and tentative into the world, it feels almost as if those garden beds will never be full. The plants, after all, grow so slow. They are hesitant to come out of hibernation or to sprout anew into the world. Weeks pass and still they are so tiny, and the days during which they will flower and fruit, when their flowers and stalks and leaves and seeds will finally grow ready to eat, seem so far away. Until one day in summer, in late June or early July, not far from the summer solstice and that longest day of the year, you suddenly realize so much of the soil has disappeared from view. The tiny plants that barely grew are much larger now and they grow so fast, every day, inching their way across the soil at an incredible rate. They crowd each other, twine around themselves, seek out sun and water and space and the chance to reproduce and continue this life they so clearly love. And it is amazing, in those moments, how different the seasons can be. It is amazing how much life blooms in those garden beds, fully present now in the world, the growing plants and the buzzing, flitting insects and the admiring, tending humans. We all come out into the sun and marvel at how refreshed the world has become.

It is in those moments that I know I am doing right. It's in seeing the insects, watching my wife, tending to our garden, admiring the flowers, eating the fruits of our simple labor. It is in picking the berries, canning the jam, feeding my friends and family and neighbors. It is in the vibrant meals. It is in the overflow of those garden boxes and the riot of color the flowers bring. While my wife and I imagine doing it a bit larger, with more control, with fewer compromises, I know that our efforts today still mean something important. I know that with each buzzing flower, every one an indication of our partnership with each other and the surrounding world.

— Portland, Oregon
July 5, 2019

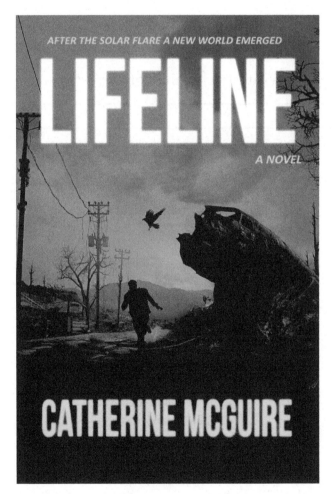

Into the Ruins is published quarterly by Figuration Press. We publish deindustrial science fiction that explores a future defined by natural limits, energy and resource depletion, industrial decline, climate change, and other consequences stemming from the reckless and shortsighted exploitation of our planet, as well as the ways that humans will adapt, survive, live, die, and thrive within this future.

One year, four issue subscriptions to *Into the Ruins* are $39. You can subscribe by visiting intotheruins.com/subscribe or by mailing a check made out to Figuration Press to:

Figuration Press / 3515 SE Clinton Street / Portland, OR 97202

To submit your work for publication, please visit intotheruins.com/submissions or email submissions@intotheruins.com.

All issues of *Into the Ruins* are printed on paper, first and foremost. Electronic versions will be made available as high quality PDF downloads. Please visit our website for more information. The opinions expressed by the authors do not necessarily reflect the opinions of Figuration Press or *Into the Ruins*. Except those expressed by Joel Caris, since this is a sole proprietorship. That said, all opinions are subject to (and commonly do) change, for despite the Editor's occasional actions suggesting the contrary, it turns out he does not know everything and the world often still surprises him.

EDITOR-IN-CHIEF
JOEL CARIS

DESIGNER
JOEL CARIS

WITH THANKS TO
JOHN MICHAEL GREER
OUR SUBSCRIBERS

SPECIAL THANKS TO
KATE O'NEILL

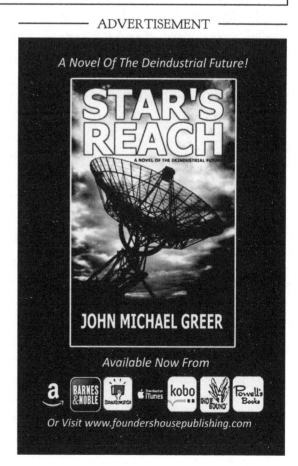

CONTRIBUTORS

JOEL CARIS is a gardener and homesteader, occasional farmer, passionate advocate for local and community food systems, sporadic writer, voracious reader, sometimes prone to distraction and too attendant to detail, a little bit crazy, a cynical optimist, and both deeply empathetic toward and frustrated with humanity. He is your friendly local editor and publisher. As a reader of this journal and perhaps other writings of his, he hopes you don't too easily tire of his voice and perspective. He lives in Oregon with his wife, whom consistently delights him.

MARK MELLON is a novelist who supports his family by working as an attorney. Short fiction of his has recently appeared in *Mysterical-E*, *Trigger Warnings*, *Infernal Ink*, and *Horror Sleaze Trash*. Four novels and over sixty short stories have been published in the USA, UK, Ireland, and Denmark. A novella, *Escape From Byzantium*, won the 2010 Independent Publisher Silver Medal for F/SF. A website featuring his writing can be found at www.mellonwritesagain.com.

AL SEVCIK is a professional photographer and author living in Tampa, Florida. His recent work can be found in two anthologies, *After Oil 3: The Years of Rebirth* and *Merigan Tales*, and in several issues of *Into the Ruins*.

DAVID ENGLAND is a ponderer, generalist, and student-of-everything who makes his home in a pleasant working-class community along the western shore of Lake Michigan, where he lives with his wife Anne, her amazing artwork, and the cacophony of voices in his head telling him what to write next. His stories have appeared in the anthology *Vintage Worlds*, the online 'zine *Tales to Astound*, as well as the quarterlies *MYTHIC* and *Into the Ruins*.

CHLOE WOODS can be found in London, writing, watching coot chicks, writing, bouldering, sneaking into the archaeology library (to do research for writing), and occasionally at her day job. Unfortunately, this doesn't involve writing. Yet. She has previously been published three times in *Into the Ruins*.

W. JACK SAVAGE is a retired broadcaster and educator. He is the author of seven books, including *Imagination: The Art of W. Jack Savage*. To date, more than fifty of Jack's short stories and over seven hundred of his paintings and drawings have been published worldwide. Jack and his wife Kathy live in Monrovia, California. Jack is, as usual, responsible for this issue's cover art. He can be found at wjacksavage.com.

VIOLET BERTELSEN is an herbalist, farmhand and amateur historian currently living in the northeastern United States. While a child, the woods befriended and educated Violet, who proved to be an eager student. She spent her young adulthood in a haze, wandering the vast expanses of North America trying to find the lost fragments of her soul in deserts, hot springs and railyards. Now older and more sedate, she likes to spend her time talking with trees, reading history books, laughing uproariously with fellow farmhands, drinking black birch tea and, on occasion, writing science fiction stories. Violet's work has also appeared in the Winter 2018 and Spring 2019 issues of *Into the Ruins* and in the old solar system anthology *Vintage Worlds* (Founders House Publishing).

G. KAY BISHOP, normally a littoteal littoral litterateur, idly sifting the shifting sands of poetry, sometimes takes a little rowboat out into the Sea of Story, and goes fishing for the Salmon of Truth, the Cod of Our Nativity, the Old Trout of Chortles or at least the Crappie of Passamenterie. In the sloping shallows just before the continental shelf drops off into the Deep, odd stuff tends to get hooked, especially when using leftover hamburger for bait. Today's catch may be bony and slight, but at least is fresh, and line-caught. Goes well with a twist of lemon or tartar sauce.

KARL NORTH was raised on a farm in New Jersey, trained to be an anthropologist but instead worked on three continents and finally started and ran a small organic sheep dairy farm in upstate New York for thirty years. Still a recovering academic, he has dabbled in systems ecology, political economy and ecological agriculture, teaching farmers and undergraduates and occasionally publishing the results on his website (karlnorth.com), in energy descent projects and in other out of the way places. He now gardens with his wife, six ewes and a Border Collie on a partially self-sufficient homestead in downeast Maine.

LETTERS TO THE EDITOR

Dear Editor,

What is the value of a horror story today? Why do you print them? Why do people write them and others want to read them? There must be a good reason that I don't understand. This is especially a puzzle to me because your readers and you are not mired in denial as so many are. I think most of us are trying to cope with the anguish of a crumbling civilization, and with nature being torn to bits to feed ever-increasing human plunder.

So why are we subjected to and why do some obviously relish fictional horror stories when daily dealing with this kind of reality? I honestly don't get it.

SM Mayfield
Port Angeles, Washington

Dear Editor and Fellow Deindustrial Fiction Enthusiasts,

The past few weeks my thoughts have turned to the history of regional writing in the United States, and what is sometimes called American literary regionalism. This style of writing became popular in the late nineteenth to early twentieth century, when it may have also been at its height, but it continues to maintain a presence in the world of letters: just think of all the Stephen King books set in Maine, or Wendell Berry's set in Kentucky. Both writers express universal themes, but the actions are played out in a place full of local color. In this style the setting itself is the eminent domain, and the writers place paramount importance on the landscape, local dialects, cuisine, customs, and history. What of the land in our future history? Surely the landscape of America will continue to exert its influence on the people who live here in diverse ways.

As I thought of how regionalism might fit into deindustrial fiction, how artists of the word might give voice to the echoes we hear whispered to us from the future of the land, I thought of how the focus on bioregions in sustainability and environmental circles, and how that might translate to literature. It was an easy step then to formulate "American literary bioregionalism."

So there you have it. A new sub-sub genre: deindustrial bioregionalist fiction. What are its aims? What are its vices? The answers are already there, waiting to be born in the stories themselves. The watersheds need speakers, the highways and roads in a valley between the mountains, having turned to asphalt gravel long ago, have new travelers. Who are they? The villages along the way from point A to point B have new architectures. What do they look like and how do the people live in them and what are their domestic arrangements? In a bioregionalist deindustrial setting these factors—and many others—should be extrapolated from what we might imagine the land to be like in one hundred, five hundred, one thousand years time—and how people might live as part of the land.

Currently writing to you from the Middle Ohio Valley, in the Miami Valley where sits the Queen City of Cincinnati.

All the best,

Justin Patrick Moore
Cincinnati, Ohio

Dear Editor,

I live in Oregon and have a good income, but I soon have to choose between leaving my home state or living on the street. Why me, us, anyone? I would not mind trying living in any of the forty-nine other states, they have got to be just as special as Oregon. But one thing I love about it is that so many disadvantaged people are succeeding in doing what society forbids them to do. The blind read, the deaf hear, the paralyzed walk, the crippled work and make a good living, and people marry same-sex partners. Meanwhile, on the other side of Planet Earth, hundreds of human beings, many of them American and some

Oregonian, are in a conga line across the Himalayas going right all the way to the top of Mount Everest. I'd be content with our dinky little Mount Hood, or at least an apartment of my own and a school for me to go to. It does not take much to make me happy. I am realistic, and most of our real world is too far beyond human reach. Any of the United States that have people pursuing their happiness like in Oregon would be what I love about that state. We are almost in the third decade of the twenty-first century! And who is making up all the rules? May everyone join me to take back our realities, unleash our dreams, and never be forbidden from anything ever again.

Rick Riffel
Hillsboro, Cascadia
Pacific Northwest USA

Dear Editor,

I have to thank Messrs. Masterson and Andreas (named after the Fault were you? My sympathies. (:-D) for their good opinions and kind care of my quivering and seismically-attuned word sensibilities. Mr. (Third Edition) Roget and I bow in your respective directions. I agree with Mr. Andreas's gracious admonition to "keep writing!" and, for my part, extend it to the rest of the readership.

I am convinced that each of you has an important story to tell; it "feels" to me that there are hundreds of stories waiting in the deindustrial ether all queued up and eager for someone to venture a pen on their behalf. I especially long to hear more of the comic side of the future; those tragedies y'all channel chill me to the core.

And no, Mr. M.: far from cavilling at your generous helping of neologisms in "The No-Account," *Into the Ruins: Fall 2018*, I thought your orthographic capture of Appalachian speech cadence and diphthongs was skillful, shock-evocative, and a delightful surtouch of verisimilitude. (I must have made up the word "surtouch"—it just seemed so *right*. But it ain't in the *Shorter Oxford*.)

Your argument for letting the language flow whither it will was most persuasive: a finely blended mash-up of meaty, new-fired slango with toasted leftovers of hobo lingo. Sort of a hearty shepherd's pie of comforting nourishment, fit for anyone who suffers from cold and rainy moods.

Allow me to take this opportunity to praise the other authors whom Joel has showcased in the past three years. Every issue that arrives makes me want to tiptoe about the house in a kind of hushed awe at the quality of the literary company I have been keeping. Every story is like a lighted buoy helping me to navigate safely through the benighted shoals and troubled waters of our times. Keep writing!

Sincerely,

G. Kay Bishop
Durham, North Carolina

Dear Editor,

A few thoughts on the predicament of decline and the approaches we can take to deal with it. I have, I must admit, a tendency to come at such things from the perspective of solution-seeking. As a mathematician/engineer by training and vocation, the basic algorithm is fairly straightforward: identify problem, solve problem, implement solution to problem, move on to next problem. Of course, while this approach works for building a bridge or constructing a power plant, it is not terribly effective when it comes to managing the deeply complex (and insoluble) systemic issues we face.

As I have mentioned elsewhere, I have served on my community's planning and zoning commission for nearly a decade now and on city council for the last two years. (I'm entering into the final year of my term, which expires next spring.) Politics, I have discovered, is nothing at all like engineering and convincing others to consider an idea or a program is nothing at all like solving a problem or conducting a power supply analysis. I've met with mixed success and generally fallen far short of my expectations from when I first took office. (Admittedly, those expectations were likely unrealistic, but that doesn't alter my emotional reaction to the roadblocks I've encountered.) I've succeeded in getting ducks added to our urban chicken ordinance. I've failed in my efforts to legalize front-yard vegetable gardening.

We have invested more in bike and pedestrian trails. But we continue to market our community to condo developers in the hopes of increasing our tax base and I still fear the threat of gentrification. My view of the future is very much in the minority on council, where the vision is about growth and development, rather than mitigation and resiliency.

Most recently, and in a different respect, I had occasion to observe my emotions regarding the limits of our individual efforts as I was getting my backyard container garden put in place for this growing season. For the past three years, I've had plots in our community garden at the edge of the city. Due to some disagreements regarding design and aesthetics, I have opted to discontinue my participation in that group and allow others who have more tolerance for the community rules to use those plots. Working in my back yard is easier, in any event. It is, however, much smaller and I admit to feeling somewhat diminished in comparison to my visions of growing rows of beans and potatoes and greens.

On the other hand, one of the messages I keep getting is to become more focused, to draw in, go smaller, and direct my efforts to my personal life rather than outward into the community and the world at large. To concentrate rather than dissipate my energy. Accepting this is one of my present challenges. The letting go of that larger scale. Being okay with this

personal path. I am not building any grand designs, solving global problems, or saving humanity by growing a bin of potatoes on my back deck.

Or am I?

David England
Two Rivers, Wisconsin

Dear Readers,

Back when I started this magazine, very early on, I received an offer of help from one Shane Wilson. I somewhat knew Shane from his prolific and at times inflammatory, almost always interesting comments at John Michael Greer's blogs, and I appreciated his offer of help. He was modest in his approach, noting that he would be happy to read stories and offer his thoughts and minor edits; I took him up on the offer and up until this issue of the magazine's run, his name has appeared on most all of them as the Associate Editor. I always appreciated Shane's insights and perspectives, on stories and the state of the world, even when I disagreed with them. He was a character, a rabble-rouser, and a unique individual whose presence in the world I always appreciated.

Unfortunately, Shane is no longer a part of this world, at least on the living plane. He died early this year, in late January. It took me a few months to realize, when I forwarded a story on to him to get his perspective only to find it bounce back to me. Finding that strange, I poked around on the internet to see if I could determine what happened and came across his obituary in a Kentucky newspaper.

Shane was still pretty young. He worked on farms and, by all of his accounts, loved the work of growing food. He often raged at the world but seemed to take a lot of joy in it, as well. He had strong opinions—those who know him from online (and I imagine in the real world) know that's an understatement—and he could offer up at times fascinating insights about our culture. He could also beat a dead horse a bit more to death, but I found that to be part of the joy of his expressed opinions.

I didn't really know Shane that well. I imagine a number of people reading this interacted with him more than I did, and no doubt those who lived and worked with him, those who spent time with him outside a computer screen, could tell you far more about the kind of man he was than I could. But from the moment I took real notice of him I always appreciated his presence. He brought a fire and passion to existence that can seem too hard to find these days. He did not spare anyone his opinion and he did not care to keep it safe. He chomped at the bit to see where the world would go next, even when he expressed disdain at its path.

I miss him and I know others do, as well. I learned of his death too late to put a notice in the last issue, and I apologize for the tardiness in this small thanks. But I did want to give this thanks, both for what he did to support *Into the Ruins* and for his contributions to this lovely and bizarre world of ours. I hope whatever life he gets next treats him well and that he takes some joy in seeing what the future holds. With luck, it will suit him a little better than the present did; regardless, I'm sure he'll have some opinions on it. I hope I'll get another chance to hear them.

Thank you, Shane.

Joel Caris
Portland, Oregon

Into the Ruins welcomes letters from our readers. We encourage thoughtful commentary on the contents of this issue, the themes of the magazine, humanity's future, and other relevant subjects. Readers may email their letters to editor@intotheruins.com or mail them to:

Joel Caris
Figuration Press
3515 SE Clinton Street
Portland, OR 97202

STORIES

FREEDOM

BY G. KAY BISHOP

"WE LIVE LIKE ANIMALS! I'M SICK OF IT! Sick to death! I hate this place and everybody in it! I wish I was *dead*!" Arnold of Lex-Eagan raged at his mother, who was resignedly extricating several pieces of freshly washed laundry from the muddy patches in the yard where they had been dragged by a pair of frisky and adventure-minded goats. It would all have to be washed again, and re-hung; and, since the radio predicted rain tomorrow, it *must* be done today. Or else some hard, cold cash would have to be paid out to the Grange Commons in exchange for some soft, warm heat generated by burning methane from the biodigesters of cow manure.

Anne of Ohio-Nan sighed and resolutely suppressed several sharp answers that sprang to her lips: "Spare me the dramatics, please," and "We *are* animals, get used to it," among them. In the Spirit, she called upon her long line of Greats and Grandmothers for patience and managed to muster a more measured and temperate response.

"Death comes soon enough without wishing for it, son. If your father were alive, he would tell you so. More than likely he would tan your britches for you if he heard you talking so wild. But you are too much a man yourself to be acting like a little boy. Go tether those goats somewhere on the other side of the field—not too far out, a big cat has been seen in the piney woods—and draw me up some water and heat it on the rocket stove in the wash-house. I have to see to the baking or we'll get no dinner. Unless you'd rather I spent your butter-and-cheese money for this week on the town laundry?"

For answer, Arnold flung away without a word said, grimly going after the goats in a purposeful manner. They skittered playfully away and he was forced to moderate his mood long enough to catch them without doing them actual harm.

He whistled to the dogs and when they came running to him, set them to guarding the two tethered goats, just in case that cat really was nearby. Looking up to him, all eagerness and adoration, the dogs could not help but mollify his flame of wrath; but it was not put out by any means. No, it was merely turned down to a low simmer, allowing a dark shadowy mood, like a brooding thunderstorm, to overspread his whole being. But he was easily able to rekindle his wrath and vent it on the pump handle; likewise, by taking a hatchet and savagely reducing a pile of kindling to flinders. The much-splintered fuel caught fire in a flash and burned hot enough to emulate Arnold's state of mind. He stuffed the soiled laundry into the big vat and tossed in a chunk of yellow shaving soap, the kind mixed with wool to make it frothier.

They had a simple boy as a hired hand, Seth of Beth people called him: his father unknown and his mother a town whore, alive but too lost to the drink to care for her own kin. Arnold set him to working the washing machine's crank handle and feeding the rocket stove—he could be trusted with the task unsupervised, from long habit and careful instruction—freeing Arnold to walk away and do something else—*anything* else!—than be what he was: a mere farm boy in a backward arsehole of a place.

He was sorry to have reminded his mother of Dad's death, but his remorse and guilt only added to his own sense of ill-usage and despair. He felt *trapped*: shut in on all sides, like a raccoon in a box, clawing helplessly in all directions without avail.

How he wished he had been born in the old days, the long ago time when men were truly free. They went anywhere they liked, as fast as they liked! They even walked on the moon! What must it have been like? To own his own car, to travel fast as a train or faster and not to be confined to the boring same-old, same-old tracks that only went from Podunk Little to Podunk Big and back again.

To whiz along the smooth roads to big cities, important business, adventures! With a beautiful blonde girl beside him as he confidently moved the wheel this way and that, sweeping the curves of the road. Glorious! Or to pilot one of those big-wheelers, moving massive loads of important goods coast to coast, getting there in record time, no plodding team of thrice-damned mules to curry, feed, and fret over harness sores.

He hated with a passionate loathing every manifestation of his staid and excruciatingly dull life. What did it matter to him that he was due this winter to move into a room of his own? It was only one of the scores of cramped little spaces arranged sow-and-piglet style around the outside walls of the big community barn-houses where most folks in town lived their whole lives. Barely big enough to hold a bed and a desk and one chair. Hell, even Thoreau had two chairs in his hut.

True, he would not have to chop wood or heat the space himself, since hot air from the kitchens, waste-burners and biodigesters was piped in a circuit from bedroom to bedroom. Everybody took a turn on the pedals to run the compressed air for the forcing fans, but that was nothing compared to hand-felling and hand-hatcheting a woodlot, already depleted by drought, just to keep from becoming an icicle. "Bicycle or icicle," the stupid twitty-twats said.

God how he hated the old women who ran the barn-houses and chattered as they bicycled the washing machines and clucked like a flock of hens over the spinning jenny that was always needing somebody to tinker with it or oil it or feed blood sacrifices to it—whatever they did in there.

And he most especially, with an enduring malice, despised the ones who organized the stupid "community dances" that were the bane of his existence. A bunch of noisy, clod-hopping clowns, while the men took their jugs outside and refused to share with anyone under age. Treating him like a moony sheep or worse. God, how he hated the hordes of screaming children who ran around inside and out, never giving a man an hour of peace and quiet. Children!

So what if a young couple he hardly knew were setting up in married life? What was it to him that some pair of pitiful suckers were settling down—very down! —taking on the duties of one or other of the lowlife little homespun enterprises that the Governors allowed them to occupy? Literally, homespun cloth or bee-keeping (considerable profit in honey and wax for careful followers of the Grange's strict rules) or what have you. The wineries, the hemp-fields, the vinegar works—bah! Canadian wheat and flax brokers, all fat and self-satisfied. He wanted none of that. It was just another kind of slavery, less laborious, maybe, than goatherding—the dregs of the food chain hereabouts—*nobody* with any kin-connections wanted *this* job when they could own cows or sheep and seek new places and new pastures—even carry clip-fed guns and fight real battles with range-jumpers!

It was only by the charity of the Grange and the Dairy Boards that his mother, widowed too soon, was permitted to maintain her homestead this far out, as if it were her own land. Which it wasn't, of course, all land belonging to the county, and leased for ninety-nine years if you were one of the lucky rich few with big families and plenty of hands for hire. Why, he and his mother could only afford a fifteen year lease, and when it was up, next year, he would have to decide what to do, where to go.

Sometimes, he thought he ought to go to be a soldier, or at least a fisherman shipping out on those big boats. Some job, some place where he could see a little bit of *Life*. Once, when he was a kid, he had seen some of those oilmen, speculators and prospectors, coming through town. The tales they told! The romance of it was alluring. But the men themselves were none too prepossessing: a scrawny, skinny lot. He compared his own long, hard-muscled arms, strong legs and lean torso with the men in his memory. It was no kind of life, that. People said they lived by thieving and begging most of the time. But hellfire, they at least got to see someplace other than this hole.

He resolutely put aside from his mind any thoughts of how his mother would get on without him when he was gone. She could sew, he airily supposed, gliding over the fact of her arthritic hands, gnarled with work; or teach, or baby mind. Something would turn up.

And he would be free! Not as free as he wanted to be, nothing like the old days; but gone for good and in for ill. Anything to get shut of this shit pit.

He kicked a pine cone for emphasis and turned to head back to the farm. He settled the bow he carried more comfortably and adjusted the quiver on his back. On the way, he collected the goats and set the dogs free from duty. They followed along for a while, then turned as one body bristling at something behind hm. There *was* something in those woods. He nocked an arrow to the string and stood still for a long time. Watching. Waiting. The sun slipped lower in the sky. Be dusk soon.

There was a faint hint of movement in the brush as whatever it was faded away into the deeper shadows under the trees. The dogs' bristles sank and they looked to him for guidance and possibly for a bit of supper.

"Come on then, let's go." They bounded away joyfully and the goats, too young to milk, also bleated for their evening treat—a trick to get them to come in on time—and they all went home.

This little incident of possible danger dispelled his ugly mood for the time being. His mother made him no reproach for abandoning the laundry chore, and he silently apologized for his long absence by folding and putting away the things hung on nails and rails around the house to finish drying away from the chickens and a possible poop-bombing by the flyover geese who passed the yard every evening on their way to their home pond. He took a big bowl of cooked food to Seth, who had his own bed in the barn-loft, where he preferred to stay with the animals who never said a harsh word to him and did not try to make him bathe, take off his boots, nor comb his hair free of bugs.

Arnold was still sore at heart and fretted in his spirit, but he was less inclined to relieve his pent feelings in an outburst within his mother's hearing. He only continued to pain her by his silent brooding and averted, sullen face.

Maybe his father would have known how to handle him, she thought; but then, maybe not. He was altogether too much like her own brothers, lank and inclined to be shiftless. Always unsettled and never reliable. He was nothing like her Lex-Eagan: a careful, precise, stolid carpenter, the pick of their generation, skilled and witty in that dry offhand way.

Her eyes filled with tears thinking of him. She turned aside to dish out the simple but filling one-pot meal that was all she had had time to prepare: baked eggs, twice-cooked beans, sour curds, a handful of garden greens and just enough milled flour to hold the mess together like a cake-omelet.

Arnold ate with an abstracted air but undiminished appetite, she was thankful to see. He polished off his plate and went back for seconds, cleaning out the pot, thank ye Gods. She doubted it would last another day; those beans and sour curds were barely on the edge of edible as it was. Tomorrow, she would bake him something nice, some treat he rarely got to taste. Like the young goats, she was hoping to lure him back into the place he belonged to.

Dinner was apt to be silent at most times, save for the blessed radio that could be counted on day in and day out. It chattered or sang or delivered solemn lectures and uplifting sermons without fail. If there was any terrific weather headed their way, they would be warned by it. If sickness or plague was in the air, the radio would get wind of it; the Committees for Safety would organize in a body and be ready to shoot infected animals or even sick people if they ventured too near.

Life, outside these bounds, was too uncertain, unsafe. Had not she lost a dearly beloved mother and husband in the struggle to get here, stay here, live a decent life? And now, it seemed, she would be losing her son too. It was bitter to think, but then truth is often bitter. Sweet delusions were what killed you before your time. Truth was medicine; if a woman had ears to hear it, she could be free. Free of worry and fear, free of specious hopes that died on the vine. Free of love that tied you to others and kept your soul from soaring. Indifference and independence were the wings of the soul. If he left, he left. That was all. She had done her best by him and everybody. Maybe it was time to do what was best for herself. Whatever that might turn out to be. She had plenty of time to think about that, later. For now, another day and another must be got through.

With just the two of them and the dogs, kitchen clean-up was quick and easy. She settled down to knit by candlelight, devoutly thankful that woven cloth was so cheap here that even a widow could afford enough for decent clothing. And the Guilds kept the quality of all dry goods up to City standards, in her opinion. No one would know, looking at her, that she was one of the poorest of the poor hereabouts.

For the next week and a half, the skies turned into a grey, overcharged sponge that just rained and rained and rained and then rained some. The ground was either soggy, boggy, or mud. The whole valley was under the weather. As the radio remarked, anyplace outside that wasn't cold and wet, turned out to be wet and cold. Anne found this backwoods idea of humor amusing, but Arnold just growled like a wet cat, and prowled around the one-room cabin like a dog too polite to shit indoors.

It was far too wet to turn the soil in the garden beds and not cold enough to bother covering the greens patches. Milking, like show business, must go on; and the twice daily trudge between house and barn wasn't pleasant. But Anne was grateful things were only wet, not icy. She was, for the most part, well-pleased to put off the outdoor chores and tend to all that wanted doing inside. Mending socks and bedclothes, patching and polishing old boots, a little knitting here, some quilting there. She even sat down to her mother's loom and wove a few more inches of the fine wide linen cloth she meant to sell at some future market to get enough cash money to buy a piglet, or even a whole side of bacon for the winter. She baked beans, pies, apples and taters; and the warm, snug little house smelled like riches and good times to her. She had known a lot worse in her parents' home!

Arnold was less content and not nearly so deedily occupied. When asked, he collected what few eggs were laid, but he did it with a set, stony face. He filled up the wood box almost to the low ceiling and chopped kindling enough to furnish a small army; but there was little else for him to do within four bare walls. Anne dared not suggest to him that he learn to sew or knit; not in the mood that hung like death veils shrouding his face. Whyever not, she often wondered: for many a shepherd and herder before him had discovered the wonders of intense concentration that knitting could bring. Many a sailor was as handy with a needle as any tailor. But not her own son.

Well, sighs and whys don't get the prize. She sent him down the root cellar to flip cheeses, turn taters and sort apples, picking out bads and counting the goods for tally sheets. He had to fodder the beasts; some of her best milkers were fussy about going out into the rain to feed.

But Arnold needed something more than light chores to keep himself occupied. She wished she could set him to dipping candles, but he was too abrupt and impatient to do that kind of work. He was too antsy to whittle anything that needed a fine touch like a niddy-noddy nor a duck decoy; but she could and did set him to striking out shingles to lay by for repairing the roofs and sides of the barns and sheds. When the heap of made shingles threatened to take over the house, she sent him out to work in the barns, which, Godd'ese knows, needed attention.

Composting and mucking out had to be done daily, but the community-built contrivances for conserving manure had long been in place and made all easy. He had only to bring the beasts out of their stalls, crank the flooring to its tilted position, then man the pump to build up water pressure and hose down the muck into the sandy drainage pits beneath the barns.

Seepage ran downhill from the pits to collect in a blackpond where the duckweed took over and throve; meanwhile the solid dung dried out for later use. Mingled with green manure of the duckweed and the black gold of the compost tea . . . well, *oh* yeah!

What made 'Tucky soils lucky soils was the best of what nobody can arrest. And no right-minded sheriff would even try. A man's gotta go when a man's gotta go. And so, dear heart, must a sheep. And a goat. And everything else that lives, shits, and breathes. Well-rotted manure, human or beast, was a reliable source of profit, most years.

But in weather like this it was no use aiming to dig out the drained dung to load into barrows nor work it into the fields. But he could keep a weather eye on the blackpond levees and open the overflow valves to lower the levels within the banks. During washouts like this, a small amount of sewage runoff was allowable (by treaty) to downstreamers whose farms might even benefit from the extra nutrients, diluted by so much rain.

Still and all, there was just not enough for a boy-man like him to do. He spent much of his unwanted spare time brooding in the corner, tinkering with the fire in the pot-belly stove, geeing it up so hot that she had to keep checking on her ovens on either side to make sure the baking did not burn.

Arnold, having nothing else on hand to hate but his mother, the goats and the dogs, chose to avert his eyes and withhold his better cheer from Anne. If he had been given something strong to drink—Lawdamercy on us! What a sorry sot he would have been. Whereas she, at her wit's end to find some way to keep him out of her hair and off her mind for a blessed minute, was just about ready to split a gut with unspoken rebukes.

All-in-all, they would each of them be glad to be soon shut of each other's company; no sound was more welcome than that of somebody's boots mounting the steps of their front porch.

They were far enough outside the safety of the Big House that Arnold fetched his gun and Anne took an atomizer of peppered vinegar into her hands, as if she was spraying for ants, before they made any move to open the door.

But their visitor called out in the voice of a friend and a neighbor, so they laid their weapons aside and welcomed whatever new trouble from outside such a visit might mean. People did not come to make casual calls out this way!

But it proved not as dire as their fears, exaggerated by isolation and close confinement, made it out to be. It was only Dirk of Mary Headway, and he had no bad news, neither sickness nor sorrow nor claims to make on their aid, save one.

First he had to be welcomed and fed with beans and carrots, an a mite of tater-sausage pie and a taste of baked apple with butter before any business could be broached. Anne bustled about briskly and Arnold came out of his broodshell and behaved almost like a human being.

"No Miz Anne, no more for me, thankee all the same. I'm full as a pig in a plum-stand. Naw'm, I wish I could, but I cain't eat another bite or I'll bust all over your nice clean floor."

The nice clean floor was considerably marred by the wet and dirt their visitor had necessarily tracked in, but a *pshaw!* and a handwave dismissed such trivialities as their guest was installed in the best chair by the stove and invited to smoke if he liked.

Instead, he took out a wad and bit off a 'baccy chew, offering the plug 'round, politely. Arnold and Anne declined but Arnold voluntarily fetched the old brass spittoon out of its corner where it had lived most of his young life.

"Nawssir, no ma'am, I ain't had too bad a ride. It's been letting up some out our way, so's I stayed dry part of the time. Not that I'm not glad to prop up a bit beside a good fire. M'hoss is in a fair way to be spoilt rotten by your Seth, out the barn. Hoss may not want to go home with me. I may have to knock your man flat to get my own hoss back!"

This joke was stretched out for a while till it looked like it was wore thin on the sole. Meaning to get the full value of a visitor, Anne inquired after several folks up at the House.

"Miz Lily ain't feeling poorly is she? Her rheumatism gets awful bad in this kind of wet. Nor your Missy Caroline—everything well? Nothing wrong with the baby coming on is there? I hope I ain't being a busybody—gets kind of lonesome out here so that my mind and my mouth both runs on."

Having satisfied her that all was well and conveyed several comfortable messages from former in-laws and delivered a pair of shoelaces spool-woven by his youngest as a kind of guest-gift (which was properly exclaimed over and praised by the recipients), there was no more Dirk could say, nor ought Anne could do to prolong the visit, so she got down to business at last.

"Well, what news you fixin' to bring us? Somethin' good and gossipy, I hope. Something that ain't fit to blab all over the radio!"

Dirk chuckled and disclaimed any knowledge of juicy misdoings.

"Naw'm, all that I came to ask is to borry your boy here for a few days, if you can spare him. Y'all know there's been a big cat roaming around Piney Ridge and stalking the meadows?"

Yes, they knew about that all right.

"Well, this here rain has drove that cat and a whole 'nother set of em to come right up to the Settlement. They ain't satisfied with hunting down no skinny old mean-fightin' razorbacks no more. Naw'm they come after Mista Murphy's pigs and got a whole mess of 'em too."

No! Murphy's pigs was the very ones Anne had her hopes sot on and she was sorry to hear of the loss. But none of the children was took, Lawd be thanked.

The long and short of it was that Dirk and several of the other men were going on a hunt, soon as the weather cleared, meaning to bring back some Flahida catskins for hide rugs and make it hot for any other cats out there who might be getting big ideas.

Nothing could have been more welcome news for either Anne or Arnold to hear. He to go off and find something or other to kill and she to have the house and goats to herself for a while.

No, still better! So's not to leave Miz Anne out here all by her lonesome, Dirk's sixteen-year old, Lainey-mae, and two of his other young'uns, Ruby, six, and Pearl, going on eight, would come out to keep her company and take up the slack on chores. If she could git Lainey to make pie crust like hern, he would be mightily obliged. And the two little squirts was wantin' to keep goats, so could she learn 'em the best ways to milk, churn and cheese?

Anne could not have been more delighted. Arnold was halfway over the moon. They were able to let their visitor go now, with no more reluctance. The roads were still too wet for the wagon, and there were no ponies for the three girls to ride, so the promised pleasure must wait a few days yet. However, just to have the prospect of a change of place and new company to welcome, it was as good as if the sun had come out shining with all his might.

Well, the weather did clear up and all was satisfactorily arranged. The wagon came laden with chattering womenfolk come to visit and a "my gracious!" plenty of supplies and provisions so as not to be a burden on the widow. Lainey turned out to be a lanky, laconic girl who brought her own 'Tucky rifle and promised to be a bit of a handful—but nothing Anne could not handle, with her goodness and cheerful common sense. And the little girls were just wild with joy at seeing new places and adoring the kids who came out of the barn skipping and ziggazagging to meet new people. All was joy and kindness, as the visitors settled in and the hunters set out.

The menfolk greeted Arnold with few words and curt, easy nods. His spirits soared to find himself among other youngsters he knew. They, like him, had been excluded from the older men's inner circles, but they just knew: they were now about to be gathered in. They had brought him an old gelding as a mount and also loaned him a tall young mule to bear his packs and ammo.

Great and not greatly different were the two species of joy felt by those who rode away and those who remained at home. Each set of companions was about to take comfort in the company of their own sex. Lainey alone was not well-satisfied with the arrangements. She looked after the troop of horse as long as they were in sight, close-mouthed and set-faced. She and her daddy had had words. When the hunters were gone, she turned to Anne, saying,

"Don't see why Ah moughtn't of gone with 'em. Ah'm a better shot than any of 'em. Eveahbody knows *that*."

"Well, love, I'm right glad you're staying here with me. I'd feel awful skeery if it was just me and Seth and these two little ones without somebody sensible and grown up, able to keep off any trouble. What if one of those cats was to break loose and come nigh the goats? We need you here, sweet-thang, a whole lot more'n those old coots and their flea-bit hounds."

Lainey's pride was assuaged and her spirit uplifted at this picture of her as a bold protector of the weak. She shouldered her rifle and came on in the house.

Later on, Anne could explain to her the other reasons why she, a girl on the verge of womanhood, was not keenly wanted on a cat-hunting expedition that was likely to be hunting for wildcats in more'n one way. Some of the facts of life about what men get up to when they go off on their own would form the topic of conversation after the littlest ones were safely abed and asleep.

Other mysteries of womanhood that she might have to face were also on Anne's mental list of little talks to have with Lainey of Marie Oakshott—the lone offspring of her wander-footed mother and nary so sweetly plump as her other kin, all from Karen Marshall. Like, if her sister died in childbirth, for one thing. And how one hoped the older men were savvy enough to hire those—to pick out the ones who weren't raddled with rash and itchcrabs and those diseases that scarred a woman's womb and all. And if they didn't, what a good woman could do to protect herself. Anne felt more needed and useful to others than she had in a long time. This would be good for them both, she believed.

Arnold came back from the cat-hunt a new and different man. Yes, they had secured some spotted hides and one of them was his very own; but so much more than that. It was not just the moonshine and drunken encounters with the hired party girls and the sleeping out under bright stars in the piney woods or the keeping watch all night with packs of too-intelligent coywolves eyeing him for a meat-treat if he didn't stay wide awake. No, it was much, much more than that. For he had also met *her*.

They had come back from the hunt after six weeks of rough living and hard drinking and general carousing. They hadn't bathed, they hadn't shaved, they hadn't been any kind of civilized for a month or more, and they all had more or less of a hangover. He and all the other lads had become close as brothers during the hunt and especially over sharing sexual confidences. Like coming back into camp, naked except for a knife, a gun and an ammo belt, with a bloody hide over your shoulder, and there to find everyone gone except a naked woman, a party girl, waiting there for you with open—and feeding you drinks and all.

Well, there he was, like a damned savage, dirty and smelling like pigs rolled in shit, and there *she* was. *She* was not the party girl he had flung himself on in the mad frenzy of the afterkill. That was a raw wound of a memory, rapidly scabbing over, soon to be forgotten. Gross, embarrassing, loathsome. *That* woman had been twice his age and she said things to him—did things to him!—that he had just as soon disremember. No, *she* was Lucilleah Landon, of the Harfordville Landons, the great cattle-running clan. *She* was a tall, willowy blonde, dressed in a cool blue skirt and pure white blouse, so she looked like she had just dropped out of Heaven, still wrapped in silky pieces of sky and cloud. She made him dizzy just looking at her.

And there *he* was—they all were!—filthy and looking like something a cat wouldn't bother to drag in. His mouth—his damned mouth dropped open and he stood there practically drooling. She looked at them, with cool blue eyes and the breeze stirring strands of her bright gold hair. No one said a word for a long time. Her eyes roved over them all, dismissing this one and that one until they rested on him, Arnold.

"Oh," she said, her voice as cool and clear as water, as cool as the rest of her was, "You must be the hunting party. Welcome to the Double-L. The troughs are that way." Then she turned on her heel and walked away. Back to the house. Even her walk was cool, her arse swaying as if in a gentle breeze.

He remembered as if in a feathery dream, how he and the men had watered their horses in awed silence. Only when the needful chore was done had they loosed their lascivious tongues, licking at her from afar and out of her hearing, each man striving to soil her perfect beauty with his own special brand of filth.

But the older men, the *real* men did not speak at all. They just looked at each other, assessing.

And Arnold knew that *they* were the ones he would have to fight to win her for himself. The others . . . ? Pffft! Still half boys. They would be no problem. Just look at them, listen to them: elbowing and ducking and wrestling each other as they splashed and whooped at the horse trough, boasting and crabbing at *her* as if they already owned her and had used her body like a rag—like those other women.

Now, as never before, Arnold was glad to be of Lex-Eagan. A carpenter's boy always had a good name. Even if that boy had never known his father for long nor learned the trade, it was in his blood. Had he not, the day before the hunt, made enough shingles to cover a whole damned shed and half a barn besides? He was made of good stuff. Women thought about things like that—it was important to marry a good provider.

What else had he to offer her? All that he had and was and would be! Only that would be enough to earn this airy spirit of all delight, this delicate bird poised for flight, this lovely woman whose net of gold had captured his heart and ensnared his soul. Songs came into his head unbidden and only the words of poetry seemed fit for speaking of her. Arnold was one hundred and ten percent in love.

Poor boy! That was the first thing Anne thought when her son's intentions became clear to her. And he *was* a poor boy in terms of his prospects, his deserving of such a rich and golden prize.

Anne, fresh from success with the gentle enlightenment of Lainey, tried her best to waken him from his enraptured dream. But what could she do? She, small, dark, plump, over forty and the fellow's mother besides, had no means to counter the potent, soul-stirring magic of this bluegrass Nimué.

She went to some lengths, still, to protect him. He was her boy after all, and it was her duty to do her best for him. She went to the trouble to unearth from the Big

House attic a sheaf of papers she had saved from his brief spell of schooling when they still lived in a kind of middle class ease, at least compared to now. He was a good hand at drawing and he had done several fancy heads of lovely girls.

She brought them back and spread them out before him. She was careful to pronounce the name of his goddess as Lu-sill LEE-uh, the way the Landons said it, instead of the lustfully slurred Loo-silly LAY-her as the boys all called her.

"Do you think Lucilleah would like you to do a sketch of her? You always had such a good hand at drawing faces." Anne was being more artful than Arnold realized. She was not really expecting him to sketch his idol's face, but subtly forcing him to recognize how different the flesh-and-blood beauty was from the beauty that he perceived within.

Arnold was silent, turning over the pages of his own work. His mother just did not *get* him. These childish souvenirs from another lifetime were not nearly good enough to win his sweet Lucia.

"No, mother," he said finally, "I do not think I ought to try. There is a fine portrait of her up at the Double-L done by Michael, her cousin. He has been studying art in the City. My work would look like a joke next to his. I had better not. But thanks for trying to help me out. I'll think of something. Don't worry." And he smiled at her and broke her heart. For she knew her stratagem had done no good.

But she *had* done some good, more than she realized. For Arnold was forced to confront reality and distinguish it from fantasy for a few hours before the enchantment re-settled on him.

Yes, he had to admit it was true: *she* was not nearly so beautiful as the imaginary girls who rode smiling beside him in his imaginary car, headed off to Californica. But she was blonde and long and lithe and he fell in love so hard it made him dizzy.

She was *different* from all the other girls around here. She had been to the City! Got a Degree at the University! She was a Doctor! He wanted her so much it hurt.

She, not averse to having a strong, handsome young man in her thrall, put aside all her family's schemes for marrying her to elegantly eligible youths from rich stock families. She bore down their opposition and married her poor little farm boy in a mist of romance against all common sense. As a substitute for a bride price, he willingly signed a contract to support her for life in her veterinary duties.

It was a reasonable bargain, all in all. He married into a wealthy family, against all odds, and she obtained a devoted helpmate instead of a maneuvering second cousin, up to all the tricks and then some. After all, if Arnold should ever prove himself to be . . . *difficult* . . . in any significant way, she could always send him away on distant, even dangerous, missions.

He had no powerful kin connections to prevent him from being expendable in a good cause. Her family were quite sophisticated in their hour of pride and circumstances—eminently sensible in such matters. She had earned her regional authority. She could divorce him if he refused to follow her orders, and if he happened to die in the field . . . well, there were others who might be willing to step into his shoes —for a suitable consideration.

The wedding took place, with all due ceremony, and the papers were irrevocably signed. Anne looked pityingly upon her son. He had made his bed and must now lie in it till death did them part—or strife and family politics. Arnold would never leave now. He was trapped in the honeypot of love, like she had been, and so many people were.

Love was all very well in its day; when you were young and strong and full of juice as a plump Himalayan huckleberry. It was only later in life when you learned what it truly meant to be free.

Willingly, Anne handed over the goats and the outpost she had made so homelike to Lainey and her kin. Lainey never married nor bore any children of her own, but her sister Caroline, who was always after men and always pregnant with somebody's get, supplied all the farmhands the place ever needed. Lainey took on the help of an older woman who had been, like her mother, a wide-ranging wanderer. Marcy had been most everywhere and suffered some and got kind of crippled in her joints. At thirty-five, she was glad to find a home.

And so, Lainey enjoyed a long spell of her own kind of love: more than most women who mate and marry and lose: one man or many, it was all the same flavor of grief. And longer by far than women who get themselves with child and into their grave all in one fell blow.

Anne of Ohio-Nan made her way into the City and her people were surprised one day to hear her voice coming to them over the radio. She read stock prices at first and ornamented her reports with pithy remarks and homely sayings that made folks everywhere look up from their chores and laugh. Anne of Nan, she called herself; she left off the Ohio 'cause that was private.

After a while, she went on to read the news and commented on that, and then the station found people got so much of a kick out of her that they put her on the Saturday night hoedown to tell stories in the intervals of the dance music.

From then on, Anne of Nan appeared on the air—an airy spirit!—for a long time, mostly on *Heart-to-Heart*: a chatty daily show, discussing the news of the day and telling stories. Some were for real, some she made up, and some were word for word stories that people from the old days had left behind.

She was no longer nobody the carpenter's widow, but a well-known personality. Arnold's rich in-laws forbore, for fear of her tongue airing any instances of misuse, to be too rough on their rough-hewn relation. He, as anyone might have predicted, soon learned the difference between being in love with a delicate bird and being married to a brainy woman who had total control over seven thousand acres of her own land; but he adjusted. He sired a couple of kids and sowed wild oats when the boss of the Double-L was acting like H– E– double hockey sticks on ice.

He spent more and more of his time out on the range, by choice; partly so he did not have to see what his new family did every day to secure financial advantage. He did not really want to know who his wife was casually sleeping with, crushing beneath her feet, or just plain ordering around. Anne's son, like thousands of cowboys before him, lived hard, worked hard, and died young.

When Anne came on the air that day, to read out his obituary, she had a comment or two to make on the subject, as she always did. People around here never forgot what she said then, nor especially how she said it.

"There was this feller once: he had one eye, one arm, one leg, and one idea at any one time. Like most of us. He couldn't see too well where he was going, but he was bound and determined to get there. Like most of us. It took a lot of time, hard work, and outside help for him to get where he wanted to be; but by the time he got there he was tired of looking at it and too tuckered out to enjoy it. So he turned around and wished he was right back where he started from. Like most of us.

"And that's life for you! Yessir, yes ma'am: that's Life, in a shelled nut."

A pause, while the studio audience laughed. Then, "Well," she said, with a catch in her usual thoughtful drawl, "I reckon there's all kinds of freedom in this old world. And the next. Enjoy what you got while ya can, folks. Godd'ese bless and good night."

SEED

BY DAVID ENGLAND

THE SOMBER SLATE SKY SUITED MY MOOD SO VERY WELL THAT DAY. Hunched forward in frowning contemplation, I sat on one of the weathered chunks of concrete refuse which lay scattered down the length of the narrow beach. Once serving to protect the shoreline from erosion, these reminders of days long past were now strewn among collapsed embankments of riprap, the storms repeatedly hurled against the shore by Lake Michigan having finally beaten down these ultimately futile efforts of human engineering to hold her at bay. As the city had withdrawn upriver, like a dying creature shriveling and shrinking into itself, repairs which would have been made as a matter of routine went undone, allowing the abandoned structures to succumb to the slow, persistent ravages of the elements.

Rather like my life, it seemed there was little point in putting forth effort anymore. All the world was heading in the same direction—right down the crapper—despite the sloganeering one heard on the radio or read in the one printed newspaper that remained in circulation in this damn county. I heard that the governor, only recently installed in Madison, had promised the return to better days would be just around the corner once the new administration's programs managed to kickstart economic growth again, if only we would all just be patient a bit longer. Easy for her to say.

The wind was up that afternoon and the water stretching out beyond the horizon showed a good amount of chop. She was a fickle thing, Lake Michigan. She could be calm as anything, placid as a pond, her surface smooth like glass with nary a ripple to be seen. Or she could produce waves that would give even experienced captains good reason to consider remaining in port. Today she was somewhere in-between: feisty, but not totally pissed. Typical for mid-spring when the lake was making that slow change from winter into summer. By August, perhaps, she'd be warm enough for sane people to think about swimming in, though I wasn't planning to be around then.

Hell, I wasn't planning on getting through that day.

The swell of the Michigan rolled toward me like an invitation, deceptively soft and gentle in the distance, before cresting to bubbling whitecaps that fell upon the sand in a harsh, uneven rhythm. It wouldn't take much, I thought. Just a bit of determination on the front end. The lake was still bone-chillingly cold. If I could make it through the first few minutes, focusing on the sheer mechanics of movement, I'd numb up quickly. Get out far enough and the cold would do its work, taking me into its embrace of false-warmth and grateful slumber. Get out far enough and there'd be no way back. That familiar knot within my chest constricted even more tightly. My eyes narrowed and I gritted my teeth. Time to be done with it.

"Beautiful, isn't she?" a voice behind me asked.

Startled from my thoughts of oblivion, I twisted around to face the speaker, looking back along the overgrown walking path I'd taken here.

The woman standing at the crest of the low sand dune was dressed like any other person one might see in these parts. She was on the shorter side, just about five-foot as best I could guess, with a slim build. Weathered jeans disappeared into hiking boots that had obviously served their owner well. The bulk of a faded brown jacket disguised her bust, though an open neck showed the red flannel worn underneath and the flair of her hips left no confusion as to her gender. A knit cap of forest green covered her head, with short, dark curls escaping at her brow and ears. At first glance, I thought her young, perhaps in her twenties, but I had to revise that assessment to some indeterminate age. Pale blue eyes regarded me with a steady, disconcerting gaze.

"She is," I agreed, trying not to show my annoyance at the interruption.

"Mind if I join you?"

Yes, I replied mentally. "Of course not," I said aloud. "It's still a free enough country."

"Thank you." She descended the dune, taking her seat on a neighboring chunk of broken concrete and depositing a small knapsack on the sand nearby. "I've been walking for a good while now and it would be nice to rest my feet for a bit."

I didn't recognize her. "You're not from around here."

"No," she acknowledged. "Just passing through, more or less."

Deciding to make the best of my thwarted day, I held out my hand. "The name's Alman," I said. "Tom Alman."

She shook with a surprisingly firm grip. "Gyre," she replied. "Jeanne-Michelle." Her head quirked a bit to one side. "But you can call me Jean."

"French ancestry?"

"French-Canadian," she agreed. "This time around, at least."

My brow furrowed momentarily at that last comment, but I let it go. Her pale eyes considered me in that odd manner of hers, quietly patient. After some time, I broke the silence that had fallen between us.

"So you're passing through, you said." She nodded in reply. "Where are you heading?"

She didn't answer right away, but continued to look at me. Then she shifted her gaze to the water. "I don't know."

That surprised me. "You don't know?"

Jean shrugged. "I go where the feeling takes me. I felt that I was supposed to come to this spot today, so here I am."

"Hmmm," I replied noncommittally. If she didn't want to talk, I certainly wasn't going to drag her story out of her. I looked back to the swells that had beckoned me only a short time before and sighed mentally. Perhaps tomorrow. Or the day after. I'm sorry, Caroline. Not today.

"I find that days like this help me to understand what it truly means to feel alive," Jean said without preamble.

On any other day, in any other place, I'd have ignored the non-sequitur and let the comment pass. But not this day. Not here. Not with her intrusion into my private grief. Nothing so contrary to my own state of mind would go unchallenged.

"I cannot agree," I replied, keeping my eyes on the surging lake. "I find it depressing. Rather like the world."

"How do you mean?" she asked, and I felt her oddly-penetrating gaze resting on me again. Looking back now, I can see how she would invite response, how she slowly and surely drew me out of myself. But that day I was in full reactive mode, blind to the path down which I was being so deftly led.

"The whole world." I gestured with an impatient sweep of my arm. "The whole world is falling apart and there isn't a damn thing that anyone can do about it."

"Falling apart?" she questioned. "In what way?"

I stared at her. "Are you mad or something?" She remained silent. "People are dying. Cities and towns are shrinking. Our technology is crumbling." I held my arms open wide. "Everything. It's all going to pieces."

Her gaze didn't waver. "And?"

No idea how to respond to that. "And it shouldn't be," I said in something of an anti-climax.

"Why not?"

I felt like a five year-old debating with his kindergarten teacher. "Just because," I replied sullenly.

She regarded me carefully. "There's more to it than just that," she observed after a long moment.

Those eyes, ever patient, invited me to tell my tale, but I resisted. Who was this woman that I should open myself, that I should bare my wounds to her? That I should talk about any of this? I looked away abruptly, back over the choppy water of the Michigan, feeling the crisp wind off the lake against my face, feeling Jean's eyes still upon me. I held off as long as I could.

"I buried my wife last fall."

"I am sorry to hear that," came the soft reply.

"It was such a stupid thing." My body tensed. "She cut herself one day as we were putting up the harvest for winter storage. It was a deep cut, but we washed it out and bought what medicine we could afford. Got infected anyway. One of those drug-resistant strains." I shook my head. "Spread up her arm. The town doctor said he needed to amputate if we were going to save her life." I closed my eyes tightly against the memory. "She died on his table."

Jean said nothing. I looked at her intently, my tone curt. "None of that was supposed to happen. Science was going to eradicate disease, feed trillions of people, take us to the stars." I waved impatiently at the lake. "Instead, the world is crumbling away, one storm-battered pier at a time. The stars are as far away as ever. Diseases are killing us that shouldn't even exist anymore. The world population is down to, what, four billion now and still falling." I glared at her. "It was all a lie."

"It was," she agreed, her voice calm.

Not exactly the response I was expecting. I had largely kept my mutterings to myself these days, but on the rare occasion that I'd spoken those thoughts aloud, I'd either been met with vacuous assurances that what we were experiencing was merely a bump in the inevitable road of progress or, more often, with a shrugging of shoulders and silence. No one, and I mean no one, had ever agreed with me.

"You appear surprised," Jean observed.

"I am," I admitted. "You say that so matter-of-factly."

She shrugged. "Why not? It's the truth, after all. The sooner we accept the fact that our society sold us a bill of goods that it was never going to be able to deliver, the sooner we can get on with adjusting to the world we actually live in."

I took that in. "So if it was all a lie," I asked after a moment, "and so obviously a lie, why was the lie told for so long?"

"Come now, Tom," Jean replied. "I've only known you for ten minutes and I can already tell that you have enough self-honesty to figure that one out."

My brow creased as I puzzled at her odd phrasing. "Most people would have said 'brains' in that context. What does honesty have to do with anything?"

"The vision we painted for ourselves," she explained, "perpetual progress, ever-expanding consumption, mastery of the environment, the planet, the universe—is a lie because it is untrue, an unobtainable fantasy. Seeing that to be the case is one thing. Admitting that fact is another thing entirely." She looked at me carefully. "The state of affairs was evident to many people many generations ago, long before now. Yet rather than admit the truth to themselves, they chose the path of self-delusion. The psychological price of admitting the truth was simply too high for them to pay." Jean looked back over the lake. "And that is why our society took the path it did, forgoing one opportunity after another to choose a more gradual and less onerous descent from the unsustainable heights it had attained."

"Stupid and arrogant, in other words," I muttered.

"Hubris is a very human trait," she replied with another shrug of her slim shoulders. "We amazed ourselves with our own cleverness. Our accomplishments were not insignificant in their own context, but we failed to put them in proper perspective."

"What you're saying," I commented, "is that we believed our own press."

"What I'm saying," she countered, "is that we fell victim to the same trap that humbles every society which develops into a complex civilization. We mistook our tools for truths and forgot that the map is not the territory."

"I don't follow."

She shifted her seat on the broken block of concrete. "Humans are very good at abstraction, conceptualization, modeling. That's why we were able to develop such sophisticated tools in the first place. But we think linearly. All of this," the sweep of her arm took in the lake before us, the sky above us, the forest behind us. "All of nature, all of the cosmos in fact, moves in cycles. Circles. Our linear models have only modest and narrow applicability. That is what we failed to understand."

"This is all well and good," I replied, fighting to keep the bitterness from my voice, "but it doesn't change the fact that my wife is dead when she didn't need to be or that the world is collapsing into a pile of shit."

"No," she responded in that odd, open way of hers. "It does not."

I shook my head sharply. "Then what good is it? What good are your circles if we can't change what is happening?"

"Perspective," she said simply.

"Pardon my bluntness," I replied, "but what the fuck does that mean?"

"Winter is coming," she answered, echoing a common saying of the times. "This is quite true. There is always a winter in the future because it is part of the eternal cycle. But winter doesn't last forever, just as no season lasts forever. After winter has run its course, there will be spring. A new civilization will send up tentative shoots into the light. Those shoots will blossom and mature as spring becomes summer. After that, the cycle will move through maturity and into decline as autumn sets in. And then, yes, there will be another winter."

"I won't live to see this spring you speak of."

"No," she agreed. "We are creatures of late autumn this time around."

"That's hardly fair," I replied sulkily.

"The cosmos gives little attention to human conceptions of fairness," Jean pointed out. "It is the greater and we the lesser. It is the whole and we are but a part.

Do you consider what a microbe in your gut thinks to be fair as you go about your life?"

"No," I admitted.

"Consider then that we are far less than a microbe with respect to the cosmos."

"That's a terribly bleak perspective of things," I observed. "You're saying that we're insignificant. That we're nothing."

She gave a knowing half-smile. "You are the one equating those two things, not me."

"What do you mean by that?"

"Exactly what I said," she replied. "Yes, we are insignificant in the context of the cosmos. It does not necessarily follow that we are nothing."

"How can be be something if we bear no significance?" I asked. "That makes no sense at all."

"Again," she cautioned with a gesture. "It is a matter of perspective. Consider a lily, a single blossom. Hardly of any great importance in the grand pageant of being, yet a thing of beauty, yet a part of the Great Dance."

"'Consider the lilies'?" I looked at her in disbelief. "Were you seriously quoting Old Scripture at me just now?"

"Why not?" She leaned back on her hands. "Yeshua knew whereof he spoke. It's just that most people couldn't hear what he was saying properly."

I'd been so caught off-guard by her reference that it took a minute longer than it should have for the rest of what she'd said to fully register. "Dance?" I asked, somewhat perplexed. "What dance are you talking about?"

She sat forward again and spread her arms open wide. "Everything. All that you can perceive—not to mention so much more that you cannot—is part of the Great Dance. Cycles within countless cycles. Spinning and whirling in an unending pattern that never quite repeats."

"Never-ending circles?" I shook my head again in not-quite-disgust. "Really? That has to be the most depressing thing you've said yet."

"How is that depressing?" she challenged in that soft voice. "I find it incredibly joyful."

"Then you're insane," I replied flatly. Her oddly-open gaze and pale-eyed patience were starting to get to me. "Round and round, going nowhere." I traced circles in the air in front of me with impatient motions. "If what you are saying is true, then what is the point? What possible purpose could there be in such a universe?"

"Oh, I can tell you that," she responded.

"Tell me what?"

"The point of it all. But it's a challenge, I'll warn you."

I looked at her, my eyes hard. "More mumbo jumbo? More vague, obtuse quotes?"

"No," she said, shaking her head. "It's quite straightforward, actually. Easy to understand." Those eyes bore into mine. "The challenge is in accepting it for the truth that it is."

"Fine." I gave an exasperated wave of my arm. "Tell me this great, mysterious truth of yours."

"Sure," she smiled in that odd way. "The point of the Dance is itself."

Abandoning all pretense of politeness, I snorted. "That," I said pointedly, "makes absolutely no sense whatsoever."

"Sure it does. Only, it's a sense that is difficult for you to accept just now."

"Explain it to me then."

"Not a problem." She shifted in her seat again, angling her body towards me. "Consider what it means when we say something means something."

I mouthed her words, working my way through the structure of her sentence. "Okay."

"When we say that this thing here means that thing over there, what we've really done is pointed from one thing to another."

I nodded slowly. "Okay," I said again. "I can follow that."

"Good," she smiled approvingly. "So the Dance is the endless end of the never-ending line. It is the thing whose arrow of meaning circles back upon itself. It is the word that is its own definition." She gestured broadly. "In the ancient construct of the cosmos as a bowl on the back of a tortoise standing on a stack of elephants, it is the elephant at the bottom which stands on its own back."

"Endless end?" I responded. "An elephant standing on its own back?" I exhaled with considerable exasperation. "That's as bad as one hand clapping."

"Let it sit for a while," she reassured me. "It'll make sense after a bit."

I didn't reply, instead staring out over the distant swells of the lake. We sat quietly for a time, the waves throwing themselves onto the sand and hissing back into that great body of water.

"How do you do it?" I asked finally.

"Do what?"

"This." I gestured vaguely at her. "What you were just doing a bit ago. This whole conversation we've been having." I waved my hand more widely. "This perspective thing."

"Oh, that." She gave me a sly wink. "I've been at it for a while now. This ain't my first rodeo."

"What do you mean?"

"Remember the cycles," she said. "Each of us has a part to play in the Dance, along with every other manifested being. Each of us is a mask put on by the One Life to play a role for a period of time. For some of us, the role is that of the wandering messenger, a caster of seeds. Tiresias. Siddhartha. Taliesin. Francis." Another of those knowing looks. "Even Jeanne-Michelle Gyre."

I looked away from her gaze abruptly, turning my face once more toward the lake. We said nothing more for a long while. The song of the waves against the sand struck me differently now for some reason, though I couldn't tell why. The quiet stretched out.

Then, with a startling suddenness, I felt that knot within me unclench. It didn't come undone, not by a long shot. But it loosened, just a tiny bit. My eyes widened at the shift in my internal landscape and I considered the line of the horizon. No answers appeared to me in that distance, but I did perceive a faint shimmering something that just might be the beginning of a sense of peace.

"Please don't take this the wrong way," I said after a time, my gaze still focused ahead, "but do you need somewhere to stay the night?" I looked back at her. "You did say you were wandering. I have a couch, if you're in need of a place. And I could probably use some company for dinner."

Jean smiled kindly. "I would welcome a roof over my head tonight, so thank you." Her eyes slid past me, further southward. "I'll need to be moving on in the next day or two, however. I'm getting the feeling that I'm needed down Sheboygan way." She looked at me directly. "The seed I was to plant here seems to have taken root."

I nodded and stood, giving the lake one final glance. Perhaps my part of this dance was to continue on for a little while yet. Perhaps, as bleak as it all seemed, there was something else to be done. Turning away from the surf, I gestured politely toward that overgrown walking path leading back toward town. "After you."

MODERN ANTIQUITY

BY CHLOE WOODS

{FOURTEENTH "READING THE PAST" SECTION;
VOLUME 37, ISSUE 3 (NODEMMER-JANOORY), PAGES 6-11}

Betha-Grace of West Yekklesheer, Deputy Editor, explores the highs and lows of material-historical investigation over the last century.

READERS WILL REMEMBER OUR REPORT in 36(4) on the Rothside bathing-house, where diggers have uncovered the first preserved shower-heads from any similar site in Bridein. The accompanying debate over whether these indicate showering took place before or after entering the water is only the most recent of a long series of controversies and intense discussion about the role of the famed—and mysterious—Classical-era bathing-houses.

Bathing-house research is a relative latecomer in the field of Classical antiquity, particularly for the Anglic territories. Not considering the work by archaeologians in the late 7th and early 8th triads, they have only really been studied since the War. Though their robustness means they are often substantially conserved, to this day relatively few sites are known, and much of our understanding continues to be based on the work at Contrawhin, Sixelms and South Cannery.

The first bathing-house site was dug at Shard Hollow in the North Bounds in 8C79, by the Old Man of Brideishi antiquity himself, Petter-Imma of Lond. Evidence of the bathing-house had been revealed during reconstruction works following the Salting, and Petter-Imma petitioned to make a record of the site before it was destroyed. (In the event, the then-unique nature of the site and its important history, including Bronze and Iron Age layers below, convinced local authorities to

INTERNATIONAL BATHING-HOUSES

Bathing-houses are not a purely Brideishi phenomenon. Similar sites have been identified across the Continent, and are reported from as far afield as Chine and the Sun Islands. The best-known are those investigated by Barcan researchers shortly before the War; unfortunately, much of their writing and several sites were lost during the conflict, and Barcan antiquity is still in recovery. There is one particular mystery: in addition to more typical bathing-houses, the Barcans reported structures they called "personal pools" (*piscina privado*) in many regions of the Med. These small, irregularly shaped external structures otherwise resemble bathing-house tins—steep-sided, tiled, and dug three or four sticks into the ground—and they neighbour presumed residential remains. Given the scarcity of water across the Med, these "personal pools" have provoked much debate. Barcan antiquitarians typically accept them as smaller versions of swimming tins and favour more symbolic interpretations, which are taken as evidence of Romance sophistication and piety. In Bridein, some express doubt the "pools" were ever water-filled at all.

to relocate the new build. The Shard Hollow bathing-house is run today as a visitor centre and museum.) Two years later Petter-Imma led excavation at a similar site, Eyarck, at the heart of the old market town known as Ebor. Due to Petter-Imma's health concerns, Eliss-Rose of Oxcrossing took over the final weeks of the dig, and was in charge when a student uncovered the famed piebald mosaic.

Fig. 1: Petter-Imma and Eliss-Rose at Eyarck. C/o Rebecca-Rose of Oxcrossing

Petter-Imma initially assumed the "bathing-houses" he'd excavated were similar to modern bathing-houses: a place to get clean and socialise. Already some, such as Bishop Birch, had argued that Classical-era people more typically had washing facilities at home, but at the time B. Birch and his peers were largely dismissed. Petter-Imma's interpretation implied a long continuity of public bathing, since comparable structures are known from the much earlier Roman period. (Not to be confused with Classical-era Romance cultures, the Romans were a short-lived but powerful people with a lasting impact on later Continental history. They ruled much of Bridein during the 5th and early-6th triad PC). Historical records confirm the Romans had an establishment much like our own, involving a complex series of pools at different temperatures to be progressed through or selected between. At both sites Petter-Imma excavated he found only single pools, big and simple, which may have hinted at a different purpose. However, a partially-obscured inscription at Eyarck, carved in the old script, was deciphered as "–bor Baths." This seemed to confirm the initial interpretation. Petter-Imma published a pamphlet on the topic and his findings in 8C81, to great acclaim.

Petter-Imma's revelation embarrassingly turned on its head when an attendant at one of his lectures the following year pointed out Arthur Goodwin's writings of the late-1st triad PC, which almost perfectly described the structures excavated at Shard Hollow and Eyarck. Rather than suggesting a bathing purpose, Arthur referred to them as *stagnum natatio*, or swimming tins.

Eliss-Rose had expressed doubts from the beginning. Born to academic parents in Oxcrossing in 8C44, she had proven intellectually precocious and prenticed to Petter-Imma at only fifteen. She became known as his star student and pioneered several important aspects of the antiquitarian method before the War. However, Eliss-Rose's name does not appear on the '81 pamphlet—despite her presence at Eyarck. She stated at the time this was down to reservations about the conclusions. She was particularly sceptical about the assumption of a courtship role for bathing-houses, which she jettisoned almost immediately in her own work as simplistic projection from modern attitudes. A year later, Eliss-Rose led the first excavations at the Contrawhin complex.

Contrawhin far exceeded anything excavated up to that point. It contains four pools of various depths and sizes, including the remains of what may be a moveable floor. Most famous is the great pool, of immense length, and bordered on two sides by a series of serried concrete stalls (then inexplicable, but now believed to be all that remain of spectator stands). As much of the original structure had already been destroyed by erosion, it was possible for investigators to dig through the underfloor layers, where they traced a long chronology including Bronze and Stone Age settlement and pre-farming flintwork.

Fig. 2: Skeletons Thet and Lam from the Bathers' Boneyard. C/o Eliss-Rose of Oxcrossing

From this excavation, Eliss-Rose argued for a very different interpretation of the bathing-houses. She claimed, boldly, that they were first and foremost a ritual space. Building on Mehmet-Jorge of Oxcrossing's ideas about the sacred role of water throughout human history, she pointed out that a purely recreational purpose seemed unlikely considering the cost to keep water heated and clean in the absence of natural cycles, and the ease (and psychological advantage) of swimming outside. Eliss-Rose acknowledged the descriptor of "swimming tin" and argued they constituted a place of worship by submersion—and swimming—in purified water. They would have been filled only on holy days.

This was fair reasoning considering what was known at the time. Part of the argument relied on the presence of human remains at Contrawhin, placed largely under the great tin, and containing as many as 324 individuals. Then judged to be roughly contemporary with the bath complex, it became known as the Bathers' Boneyard, and served to shore up arguments the complex had been built over a holy spot, incorporating aspects of death and afterlife rituals into the hypothesis.

Not everyone agreed. Rebecca-Rose of Oxcrossing, in an act some took as a rather dramatic form of teenage rebellion, published a contradictory interpretation of the Bathers' Boneyard the year after the Contrawhin dig. Considering the mismatched alignment with the bathing-house and the gravesite's extension under a contemporary theatre, she suggested there was no real link between the Boneyard and the bathing-house. An association between water and death would not match either Mehmet-Jorge's theories or the known pre-Classical and Classical-era traditions of cremation and baptism: the first, incorporating death in fire, which is the opposite of water; the second, placing water at the centre of rituals focused on birth and renewal.

A few years later (8C88), Petter-Imma passed away peacefully at the grand age of eighty-three, still holding fast to his original interpretation. Most others in the field now agreed the bathing-houses had been places of ritual rather than bathing (though the name "bathing-house" stuck; despite Eliss-Rose's best efforts, the more accurate "swimming tin" has never caught public imagination), and perhaps belonged among the well-known suite of monumental and prestigious architecture belonging to the pre-Classical and Classical era. Some pools were certainly of breath-taking size: the diggers did not reach the end of the great pool at Contrawhin until the fourth year of excavation, when it was finally revealed to measure 87.4 sticks (or four and a half Lond tram cars).

Fig. 3: Sketch of a late Anglic house with "bathing room" clearly marked, from Abbesdon, under Laurel-Tifan and Moyra-Caro, 8C87. C/o Moyra-Caro of Highborough

The main opposition to the "ritual" school—and marking a break from the Symbolist path of antiquity altogether—arrived in the form of Moyra-Caro of Highborough and the Lord Archer's Fields dig opened in 8C91. Older readers might also remember this as the year they first heard about the new technique of carbon dating, to become influential shortly down the line. Moyra-Caro was the student of no esteemed scholar and, largely self-taught, had spent years—as she puts it—"paying my dues in a corner of history nobody was very much bothered about." The corner in question was the post-Classical period often nicknamed the Dull Ages, where she continues to maintain an interest, and where much of her early work alongside

---

HISTORY'S RICHEST CIVILISATION

As antiquitarians, we often focus on the similarities between ourselves and people in the past, as otherwise it is easy to start thinking of them as legends or unusually clever animals. The Classical Anglics in particular have been held up as a civilisation much like our own. It is true they were widely literate, practised a form of democracy (involving "elections"), and pioneered many of the technologies we depend upon today. But the differences are equally many: they were monotheistic, partially monarchic, educated their youth in standardising institutions (*scholarum* and *collegium*) and happily let the poor starve before employing a system of indenture. Their concept of economics depended heavily on complex (and, from what has been deciphered, frankly superstitious) financial theories; any theory of energy flow was embryonic at best in the later Classical era. Equally, they had no notion of the Balance, and rarely paused from interfering with natural systems despite repeated evidence of poor outcomes. These twin facts have long seemed at odds with the period's apparent success, and only more so since antiquitarians entered the field: nearly every finding over the last fifty years has shored up historians' long-standing claims that Classical-era people—globally—lived individually wealthy lives in numbers not seen before or since. It seems only possible to conclude they benefited from a stunning energy glut unavailable to or unusable by earlier and later people. That is to say, they did not have a theory of energy flow for the same reason a tree has no word for wood. The source of this glut remains a mystery, and proposed explanations have included intensive geothermal tapping, use of a now-depleted fuel reserve (such as uranium, helium or a carbon compound), a temporary surge in the sun's solar power, or alien intervention.

---

then-partner Laurel-Tifan of Mowbrey paved the way for the recognition of the "Dull Ages" as far more mutable and sophisticated than had been previously assumed. By the time she waded into the bathing-house debate to take on a bastion of Brideishi antiquity, she had become known in that close-knit community as an antiquitarian of good sense with a knack for spotting the obvious-but-overlooked conclusion. Beyond the narrow post-Classical sphere, though, many doubted her credentials, particularly as an early champion of the Pragmatist path then just beginning to challenge the earlier, dominant Symbolist path Eliss-Rose and her peers subscribed to.

Where those following the Symbolist path had largely focused on communal spaces and burials, Pragmatist acolytes were known for their interest in residential homes. By 8C91, work led by Laurel-Tifan and companions conclusively showed that the Anglics had indeed, for a period of several centuries at the height of their civilisation, constructed individual washing facilities in almost all homes. This revelation fell among a number of others—such as the space mission papers recovered from the Ousaviick Archives—demonstrating the almost unfathomable wealth of energy the Anglics and others of the Classical world had available to them, and silenced the earlier argument they would not be willing to expend great resources on "mere" recreation. The increase in pool sizes well into the late-1st triad PC (the currently agreed-upon date for the construction of the great pool at Contrawhin), congruent with other indicators of steadily rising fuel availability, only served to reinforce the point.

Moyra-Caro based her initial claims around the dig at Lord Archer's Fields, an unremarkable one by bathing-house standards. It boasted a single standard large pool situated at the centre of a small series of concrete housings and, though well-preserved, might have been thought to offer no particular insights. It was for this very reason Moyra-Caro opted to use it as a case study: she introduced the '91 pamphlet with a reminder that the typical may be more instructive than the unusual.

Working from first principles, Moyra-Caro argued the bathing-houses had been no more and no less than places to swim. Though they may seem shockingly wasteful to contemporary eyes, by Classical-era standards they were really fairly modest, and would have provided swimming facilities to those who could not reach them —which, contrary to Eliss-Rose's (perhaps rather well-off) assumptions, are not always easily accessible today.

Fig. 4: Rebecca-Rose, far left, exhibits pied ware at a site tour of Sixelms while Moyra-Caro, second from left, delivers her a hot drink. C/o author

The pamphlet, *On the Social Role of So-Called Classical-Era Bathing-Houses*, caused quite a stir. Six subsequent years of argument in various publications—including *Modern Antiquity* Issue 9(2), 10(3), 12(1) and 12(2)—came to a head when Moyra-Caro presented a lecture reporting on the Sixelms site at the Oxcrossing Antiquitarian Series of 8C97, which Eliss-Rose and Rebecca-Rose both attended. (It likely did not help matters that the report on the Svannian circle-glider had fired up debate about Classical-era sports only weeks earlier.) There Moyra-Caro set out her hypothesis once again. When Eliss-Rose retorted that the Lord Archer's Fields bathing-house and two other probable sites were situated near the sea and therefore redundant recreationally, Moyra-Caro stood her ground with the suggestion they might have been used in winter, since the Anglics did not share our concept of seasonal balance. The argument escalated until, as one witness reported, "Reb had to hold her old mum back 'cause she thought Ellie was about to lay hands on poor Moyra." Moyra-Caro maintained her composure but remained verbally obstinate; five people in total were evicted from the lecture hall; and the antiquitarian establishment suggested both women were suffering from a failure of collaborative spirit.

Eliss-Rose, at least, showed no inclination to make amends. She published in a number of journals, arguing: that size inflation also fitted with a ritual purpose, and perhaps a sense of monumentalism; that the Anglics might not have explicitly understood seasonal balance, but they cannot have been immune to seasonal cycles more generally, as no living people studied by anthropologists are; and that the holy role of water had not been contradicted. For a *coup de grace* she pointed out that Classical-era people may have been rich enough to take baths and cook at home, but this did not mean every small town could afford to heat half a million litres of water each day, or even for half the year, simply to *swim* in.

While Eliss-Rose doubled down, her daughter had come to another conclusion. A few months after the lecture, Rebecca-Rose wrote a segment for *Industrial Archaeology* in favour of Moyra-Caro's position and reporting new age estimates via carbon dating for the Bathers' Boneyard. Biological material immediately under the great tin, including a cat skeleton and several small rodents, dated to the early-1st triad PC, but the skeletal remains from the Boneyard were at least four hundred years older. Of course, this did not totally undermine the prospect of ritual: Rebecca-Rose herself had suggested symbolic possibilities which excluded the Boneyard several years earlier. But it demolished the already-fragile confidence the antiquitarian community had in Eliss-Rose's assertions.

That summer, Rebecca-Rose joined the Sixelms dig for its second year, as partner to Moyra-Caro.

Sixelms is less impressive than Contrawhin, but it is nonetheless a large and critical site. It has three tins, two fairly typical—one standard large, one smaller—the third surprising. Pool B, as it is known, was the first non-rectangular pool to be uncovered in the Brideishi Isles (it looks roughly as if someone had lopped two corners off a square, giving it six sides), and the research team soon established that it was unusually deep. It took two years' digging to reach the bottom, and Moyra-Caro and Rebecca-Rose finally concluded that Pool B had exceeded 7.8 sticks in depth. This is far deeper than any person might need to comfortably swim in and antiquitarians are still stumped about its use.

Fig. 5: Trevor-Eeli's climate graph, 3rd triad PC to the present day. Copied with permission

Up to this point, all interpretations of bathing-houses had rested on a single, unquestioned assumption: that the people of the Classical era would, like ourselves, swim outside on a regular basis. Eliss-Rose had contested the tins were hardly used. Moyra-Caro suggested they would be used where open water was not freely available or suitable, and that this occurred more commonly than initially presumed, but she never supposed anything other than frequent outdoor swims during the spring and summer months. The first inkling this might not be the case hailed from a research programme entirely unconnected to antiquity.

In the year 9A03, Trevor-Eeli of Doublelinn released a report on historic and prehistoric climate patterns taken from sea core drilling. With apologies to the historians, who'd been arguing for climate shifts since the Dull Ages (e.g. Meror of Sutherall's treatise, *The History of the Britons*), the antiquitarian community began to accept the stunning evidence that the Brideishi Isles had been three to five natural degrees colder, on average, during the Classical era. Modelling (and historical reports) suggested they would have been particularly cool and wet in summer. While swimming might have remained possible, at least for hardier individuals, it would only have been *pleasant* for a minority of days across a short stretch of the year.

But if that seemed to prove the point about usage, what of Eliss-Rose's and others' comments on the standardisation of tin sizes, the presence of at least two unusually deep tins at Sixelms and a second site, Eden Bay, and particularly Arthur's description of "Olympic" tins? A simple substitute for outdoors swimming might justify the presence of heating indoor tins, but it hardly explained their consistency of form. All tins excavated, except the deep tin at Sixelms, were perfectly rectangular. A majority were precisely 43.7 sticks long. The patterns of tin markings at Eden Bay confirmed the use of *angiportum*, or "alleys," suggested by the pied ware recovered from earlier digs.

THE MALARIA PROBLEM

The relationship between malaria and Classical bathing-houses offers an enlightening example of our own historical myopia —and the possible impacts of antiquitarian research in the present day. Caution regarding diseases such as malaria, yellow fever, whitelips and other hazards of bathing in or spending any length of time near stagnant water is so entrenched in our culture, antiquitarians did not even recognise their assumption that all Classical-era pools must have been built indoors to evade insect-borne disease (whatever other considerations of weather, ritual, and monumental architecture were involved) until it was challenged. Brideishi researchers first learned of possible outdoor examples only when free communication was restored and Barcan antiquitarians passed on their reports of "personal pools"; the risk of insect-borne disease forms one argument against their use for swimming or washing. However, as Trevor-Eeli proved, the world can change as much as our societies. A much-degraded but unambiguous outdoor tin in the Fens (see *Modern Antiquity* Issue 35(4)) has provoked reassessment, and adds weight to growing evidence that several now-widespread insect-borne diseases were virtually unknown in Bridein, and possibly across the Continent, during the Classical era. Pro-eradication organisations, notably the Healers' Central Group, have jumped on these findings as evidence it may be possible to control or fully wipe out various diseases (in particular malaria, which they describe as a "scourge"). So far no assembly has taken action but, whatever the arguments against meddling with the Balance, it will be difficult for anyone who has watched a loved one succumb to malaria or whitelips to consider their extinction an undesirable outcome.

This alongside a growing understanding of the Classical-era focus on competition, and particularly athletic competition, suggested it was not so much inaccurate as it was underselling the point to write the bathing-houses off as places of "mere" recreation. To the Anglics of the Classical era, particularly in the final centuries, athletic recreations (*ludi*, or "games") were highly ritualised and may have been viewed as almost holy, and absorbed many of the social functions of religion proper —which had been somewhat truncated in the later Classical period.

This suited Eliss-Rose, though she may have anticipated a more explicitly divine role. She continued (and continues) to maintain, per Mehmet-Jorge, that all bodies of water large enough for submersion can be considered somewhat sacred—in our own society as much as the Anglic—and we cannot write off the construction of the swimming tins as a neutral act, bereft of symbolic meaning. However, she conceded, the Classical-era bathing-houses may have been *perceived* as primarily mundane rather than ritual spaces and used not infrequently. Moyra-Caro too showed herself willing to compromise, with the comment (interview in *Modern Antiquity* 24(2)) "She might be right. All that semiotic stuff gives me a toothache." In 9A09 Eliss-Rose teamed up with Rebecca-Rose and Moyra-Caro to publish *Bathing-Houses and Open-Water Swimming in the Classical Era*, adding theoretical depth to their years of well-ordered site reports. Though poorly received by adoptees of the growing Parsimonian path for its neglect of structural dynamics and over-complication, the longform presented the nearest to consensus on the topic ever achieved and appeared to settle the most critical issues.

But the digs at South Cannery that summer held a further shocking revelation.

Nobody had expected South Cannery to be a remarkable site. A standard 43.7-stick tin inside a backfilled bathing-house, now buried under the foundations of a Dull Ages barn and a set of pre-War public offices scheduled for demolition at the outskirts of Brisolton, it might not have been excavated at all but for Brisolton's longstanding historical rescue programme. Rebecca-Rose pulled together a team of volunteers and students for a six-week dig in late spring before returning to Moyra-Caro at Sixelms. Then chemical analysis of the tiles identified something astonishing: chlorine residue.

Fig. 6: The reconstruction swimming tin in Fairport, currently closed for renovations. Based largely on Lord Archer's Fields, the most complete individual bathing-house, it is 43.7 sticks in length and holds 437,000 litres of water. C/o Fairport Temple Historical Centre.

The question of water safety had been a pin in the side of bathing-house research since the beginning. How could such a vast quantity of water be cycled, or kept clean? One model suggested boiling, another that purifying plants were grown inside the tins, a third that the water was simply replaced frequently: but no evidence to support any of these models had been found. On the other hand, Classical and early Dull Ages writings took note of that era's fondness for disinfection, decontamination, and other direct methods of killing micro-life, regardless of the effect on local humans. Household cleaners were renowned for their mortality rate, and the ideal space, according to some writers, was one in which no bacteria lived at all.

Rebecca-Rose and Moyra-Caro incorporated the presence of chlorine into a modified version of their earlier hypothesis to suggest swimming tins had not been used simply when better outdoor options were not available, but—bearing in mind this Classical-era fear of nature—as a preferred alternative. The poisonous chlorine had, they suggested, been used in a purification (sic) ritual to ensure the safety (sic) of the water.

The conversation of the last few years has therefore returned to the initial idea of hygiene. At present, and in keeping with the single-solution frameworks favoured by the Parsimonian path, it is generally taught that Classical-era bathing-houses existed to provide a place to swim cleanly, when outdoor spaces were considered unclean and unsuitable. (Among the long screeds now being published on the anthropological significance of the binary dichotomy between "natural/man-made" and "clean/unclean," we must not forget the Classical era was a time of severe environmental pollution, and many outdoor bodies of water would have been legitimately hazardous.) Secondary considerations may have included weather and standardisation for competition purposes, while a more intrinsic symbolic role likely underlay any and all explicit motivations. Work continues at sites such at Rothside, Sixelms and Tayend Bridges and, though we have working answers to several major questions, these curious buildings no doubt have much more to reveal about their role and purpose in Anglic society.

Bathing-houses have long caught the public imagination as hallmarks of Classical grandeur and decadence, so it is my pleasure to announce that the reconstructed swimming tin in Fairport will reopen at the end of Nodemmer following repair works. It will be open to the public for viewing throughout the year. If you do wish to swim, please be aware the tin is filled with solar-heated water on the first El-day of the month (March through Tobber) and remains open for a week. Rest assured no chlorine or other impurification methods are applied. The visitor centre received a Commendation of Educational Value for the years 9A20 and 9A21, and is well worth a trip.

THE FIRST TRAIN TO TAMPA

BY AL SEVCIK

A STEAM LOCOMOTIVE! THE KIDS HAD NEVER SEEN SUCH A THING. First, the kids huddled. Then in a tight cluster they inched forward and cautiously circled the strange machine. Suddenly the bravest, a thirteen year-old girl, ran up and slapped her hand against a black iron beam that connected the two driving wheels with the piston. At that moment a safety valve on the engine's boiler opened with a loud hiss, shooting a cloud of steam and spray in the girl's direction. The cluster disintegrated. Several kids screamed. The gutsy girl jumped backwards and fell sprawling in tall grass beside the tracks. The steam vanished and the girl looked at the other kids and laughed.

Most of the adults hadn't seen a locomotive either, except for the handful that had traveled north to the Florida panhandle and been to the museum in Tallahassee. The adults stood safely back from the hissing, steaming contraption. A couple chatted with its driver.

Jason felt a nudge to his ribs. "Hi, Beth."

"You did it, Boss. I mean, Mr. Mayor. Jason. Right here, standing in front of us, is the first train Tampa's seen in a hundred years, maybe even a hundred and fifty. And it's really here right now, all thanks to you." Beth raised her hands and adjusted the black ribbon taming her shoulder-length red hair. She punched Jason's arm. "Come on, celebrate! Climb up into the cab and give us a speech."

Jason ran his fingers through short-cut black hair, his black eyes surveying the gathering. He nodded to recognize an approaching heavyset man with salt and pepper hair. "Good afternoon, Tim."

"Don't say 'good afternoon' to me, you crook! If I had my way these folks here would be strapping you to that cursed engine and sending both you and it back north to Tallahassee, to any place, just to get rid of you. Damn fool. Spending the town's money on this show-off scheme. What were you thinking?"

Jason struggled to hide his exasperation, to keep his voice calm. "What am I thinking? Tim, I'm thinking that this locomotive has pulled two cars to our town. One car is loaded with more coal than two dozen horse carts could bring. The other is a boxcar that will go back loaded with iced fish and fish fillets from Tampa fishermen for the markets in North Florida. Fish that will be for sale in Tallahassee tomorrow. Fresh seafood from Tampa Bay delivered in one day instead of a week!"

Tim's face reddened. "You're a crook, Jason. And stupid. Stupid not to see the danger. Sure the train can take fish north to Tallahassee and even up to Old Georgia. But it can also bring soldiers and bureaucrats to Tampa. You know they'll come and they'll take over everything we have. I'll get you thrown out of office if I can't get you jailed." Turning away, Tim disappeared into the crowd.

Beth's eyes were wide. "Wow! That was quite a lecture. What are you going to do?"

Jason sighed. "Nothing. I don't blame Tim. He's been shipping fish north in his dozen horse carts and he sees that won't work any longer. He's afraid for his business." Jason glanced at the sun, now slipping behind tree tops. "Sunset soon and I'm not near ready for the day to end."

Two men ran up to the locomotive and shouted, "Watch out, move away folks! It's going to back up. Somebody get those kids out of the way."

A switch was thrown and the engine backed onto a siding that sloped up and over the top of a partly buried topless concrete box. Several men attached thick ropes to the coal car and then to three heavy-duty winches normally used to pull up boat anchors. The engine backed the car partway up the inclined track. The car was decoupled and the men strained to crank the winches' hefty gears, which inched the car up the sloping track to a spot directly above the open box. One man climbed onto the car and pulled on a large wheel connected to gates at the bottom of the hopper car. With the sound of metal sliding against metal, the bottom of the car opened, letting loose a waterfall of coal into the concrete container and creating a thick gray cloud of coal dust. Fortunately the cloud rose into an afternoon breeze that whisked it away. The empty car was eased back down and re-coupled to the boxcar, which was still attached to the locomotive.

While this happened, crews loaded containers of ice and fish into the boxcar. The sliding doors were shoved shut and a man waived to the engineer. The engine and the two cars moved back onto the main track, this time facing away from Tampa.

Kids and adults stood together in afternoon shadows watching the smoking, steaming apparition move away from them until the track curved and the train disappeared from sight.

‡‡

Most of the townspeople had walked the mile from town center to the rail tracks and the adults now drifted back in small groups. Their entertainment over, the kids crowded together and ran ahead like swarming bees. Jason walked away from the crowd, pass the newly filled coal bin and over to a grove of oaks where he his pickup waited. He had left the pilot flame burning to keep water in the auxiliary boiler warm. He pulled a small lever on the dash to activate the big burner, waited four long minutes for steam pressure to build, then headed back towards town but, on impulse, turned off the direct road onto another that followed Tampa Bay's serpentine shoreline.

At high tide the bay was beautifully inviting but twice a day the waters moved away and exposed ragged structures of ancient concrete and metal, ghosts of the Historic Tampa that had thrived here in the unremembered long ago before the globe's energy cratered and before great ice sheets slid off Greenland, or the South Pole, or wherever, causing the Florida coastline to shift inland. The forlorn and broken buildings were homes now to fish and crabs.

In spite of the long shadows, Jason steered his steam-powered pickup off the gravel road onto roadside grass, killed the alcohol fire under the boiler, and stepped out of the truck. Facing Tampa Bay and the sunset's deep red afterglow, he pressed an index finger against each side of his forehead and whispered, "Mighty Mollusk, protector of the bay, thank you for the food of the sea and the fruits of the land, and I specially thank you for allowing the locomotive to come today to Tampa. Protect our town and all who live therein."

For two minutes more he stood quietly contemplating the remnants of the old buildings that seemed to beckon from the sea. For what? To be somehow saved from the deepening water? To be returned to times past? He raised his eyes to the darkening sky and let his mind create ephemeral visions of what was and what might have been.

Jason's calm turned into annoyance as the grass around him suddenly illuminated and a steam sports car, its metal frame and wood body painted glistening red, pulled onto the grass just ahead. Beth, her red hair streaming in the bay breeze, jumped over the car's low-slung door. She paused, faced the bay, briefly touched fingertips to temples and then ran to Jason. "Might be trouble coming, Mr. Mayor."

"If so, Beth, I'm sorry you found me."

She didn't smile. "We just received a Morse-message from Mayor Castro in Orlando. He and the mayors of New Miami, Sarasota, Lakeland and Ocala are furious at you for fixing the tracks and bringing the railroad back. They say that now all the towns in South Florida will be dominated by Tallahassee. Apparently a group has been sent to talk to us." She paused and waived a paper. "They say 'talk,' but something tells me that's their word for trouble."

Jason thought a moment. "I wonder why they didn't they include the mayors of Jacksonville and Gainesville?"

"They're more to the north. More used to Tallahassee. Probably those mayors are waiting and watching to see what happens."

"Maybe so. As for us, you may be right, this could be a problem. If armed visitors are coming at us from the south and east we should receive Morse-message alerts when they pass close to the towns that partner with us. In any case, it will take them at least a day to get here, maybe two." Pausing, he looked up at the stars for a moment. "I was headed home but instead I better go to the office to prepare."

Beth turned away.

He watched as she walked back to her car. "Uh, Beth . . ."

She turned and stood facing him, hands at her sides.

A dozen thoughts raced through Jason's brain and a dozen feelings pulled at his emotions. The world warped. It seemed as if he was immersed in an artwork, an enormous oil painting that contained all the land and sky. Moonlight sparkling in the rippling waters of the bay, Beth standing beside her car, hair falling over shoulders outlined by moonlight, her face softened by the night's glow. All created by a master artist. He lifted his hand to reach for her but stopped, dropped his hand and buried his thoughts, remembering his self-promise to stay true to the memory of Mary.

"Did you say something?"

"Nothing, Beth. Nothing."

She nodded.

"Uh, Beth . . . last night at the community dance, there was a . . ."

Beth interrupted. "A brown haired girl with green eyes, freckles and an overly cute nose." She studied his face. "Am I correct?"

"I didn't notice all that stuff."

"Sure you did. But as you've asked, her name is Susan, she's from Orlando."

Jason looked away, hoping he hadn't blushed. "Thanks. Just curious. You know, checking on a stranger in our community."

"Mr. Mayor . . ."

He looked back at worried blue eyes.

"Careful, Boss. The word is that she left just ahead of the Orlando police. There's a second message on your desk. Orlando's asking for her back. She's a felon."

‡‡

Jason eased his steam pickup from the grass to the gravel and continued along the winding bayside road. Sandy coves along the coastline protected fishing craft whose rainbow colors turned to pastel grays in the increasing gloom. Now the boats rested on beach but were anchored by ropes to the upper shore in deference to the next high tide. Soon he came to the cluster of tackle stores, taverns and eateries that made up downtown Tampa.

Vegetable oil lanterns twinkled from windows, competing with the fireflies' random sparkling of the dark countryside that rose behind Tampa. The row of taverns and the groceries and seafood shops along Main Street glowed a soft yellow from the dancing oil flames. Jason noted that Fred had already turned on his latest invention, the town's experimental electric street light. Janson smiled. *Fred might be a boring nerd but single-handedly he's dragging Tampa into the twenty-third century. What we really need is a way to make cheaper electricity. Bringing coal in by railroad will help.*

Jason turned the vehicle's single front wheel, slowed and steered to the road's edge. He stopped the truck and studied the flickering lights of the town. The vegetable oil lanterns were pretty but the town needed cheaper oil for lighting and to heat the fishing boats' boilers. Making hemp oil with the extraction machine Fred had built would be a good beginning but it didn't produce enough for the town's needs, and was too expensive. Fred promised to improve the process, though, and Jason hoped he could.

A quick knock on the car's side panel jerked Jason from reverie. "Mr. Mayor, Jason, I thought it was you."

"Oh, Bishop Brody. Good evening." Framed in the opposite window was a blond-haired man in dark pants and an off-white jacket with a wide, light-blue collar. He carried a polished stick with eight ribbons of different colors attached to one end. The ribbons represented the eight arms of an octopus and also the eight major virtues.

The bishop's eyes bore into Jason's but the corners of his mouth betrayed a small smile. "I hear the Orlando police are grumpy because we have their lady."

Jason grimaced. "Who's handling Morse-messages today? April? That girl is impelled to tell everyone everything she knows." He opened the vehicle door, got out and walked around the car to the bishop. "We've got some angry people from South Florida coming to visit us. I don't know what to expect. Darn it, I really need to work at my farm this evening but I've got to go back to the office."

Bishop Brody said, "I'm sure it's tough managing a town's business in addition your own. But the pay is good, right?"

"Yeah, sure. Payday script from the Tallahassee Currency Bank. They tell us the money is backed by gold they've hidden in a secret vault. We only have their word for that. The money could be just ink on paper but as long as people have faith in it . . . Of course, I sometimes get real stuff, a gift chicken or cut of beef, but more often than not the gift is an obvious bribe."

Bishop Brody raised his stick, twirling it so the eight ribbons fanned out in a circle. Raising his head he addressed the air above Jason. "Mystic Mollusk give this man to realize that he is loved and appreciated more than he knows, and imbue his soul with the strength he needs to do this difficult work."

Jason held out his hand and shook the Bishop's. "Thanks Mike. I appreciate that." He walked back to the other side of his car. "See you soon."

"Hope so. Surprise me and come to Monday services." He waved as Jason steered back onto the road.

Jason parked next to city hall and walked across the shadow-enveloped street to a lighted tavern and bought a fish sandwich. Then back to city hall. He stopped. Something about the shadows near the entrance . . .

A woman stepped into the moonlight. A soft half-whisper: "Hello, Mayor."

"Hello, Susan Smith."

The whisper again. "You know my name. I think you better come nearer and share my shadow so no one will see you talking with an escaped criminal."

"You're judging yourself harshly."

"Not if you ask the folks in Orlando."

"I know Mayor Castro. He would control every detail of the whole universe if he could. But right now you are a guest of the town of Tampa. I'm willing to leave it at that." As his eyes adjusted to the shadow the details of her face and short cut brown hair came into focus. He was caught for a moment by her green eyes, then mentally shook himself. He turned away.

"Before you go, Mr. Mayor . . ."

"My name's Jason."

"Jason then. The mayor, the folks in Orlando . . . You don't have friends there. I overheard things about the men they are sending here. That's why they didn't want me to leave, why they were going to put me in their jail." She vanished back into shadow.

Jason unlocked the main entrance to city hall and stepped into a dark hallway. He walked cautiously until he reached a familiar door. To his surprise it was unlocked and his office lanterns lit.

Beth stood at a worktable sorting papers. "You said you'd be coming back to your office. I thought you would welcome some help." Her red hair, now gathered into a ponytail, swept back and forth across her back as she moved.

Jason felt the impact of her blue-eyed gaze. "You don't need to do this, Beth."

"But I want to. You do so much, managing your sheep ranch plus this town with its crisis-a-day. I'm happy to help you."

"I guess I asked for this," he said. "After all, I did run for election."

She batted the air. "You were the only good guy on the ballot. The whole town thought so. That's why you got eight out of every ten votes."

Why was she so attractive this evening? He pushed the thought aside, saying, "Actually, I can use your help. First thing tomorrow would you contact the council members? I'm calling an emergency meeting. Let's make it at one o'clock. Also, help me choose three council members to join me afterward. I'm worried that excitable folks from other towns may try to harm the railroad. I'd feel better after a ride along the rails for a few miles. Just to check."

"Uh, boss . . . On your desk. There's another message from Orlando."

He picked up the sheet of paper. "April's printing. Always perfect." He read aloud. "'From the office of the mayor, Orlando. To Tampa Mayor Jason Roberts. Jason, my friend. I'm asking a favor from you. A young woman named Sally Smith left here a few days ago and word is that she's in Tampa. It's important that we have her back. I would much appreciate it if you could hold her for us until I can get someone there to claim her. Regards. Miguel.'"

He looked up to meet Beth's eyes. Again, her steady, strong gaze. His chest, his heart, something inside him warmed.

She said, "Are you going to lock up Sally? Put her in jail?"

Jason held the message against his chin, thinking, then he dropped it into the waste. "No. Sally Smith is a guest in our town. We don't lock up guests without a reason, and Miguel didn't give me a reason."

Beth exhaled audibly. "Jason, I admire . . ." She took two steps towards him then stopped, her hands palms up.

"You and I, we have worked together for quite awhile, Beth."

Her answer was immediate. "One year plus eight months and fourteen days. I volunteered to help in this office a month after . . . after your wife's spirit was called back to the sea." She paused. "I miss Mary."

Jason looked down at the table. "I do, too." He watched his finger trace repeated circles on the table top. "I'm still struggling to untangle my mind, to figure out what's past and what's now. I feel I have to honor Mary's memory, but I'm not sure what that means."

"My guess is that it means to continue to live your life as the good person that you are."

He raised his head and looked at her, her hair, her face, his eyes traveled down her body. "Beth I . . ."

"Yes, Jason?"

He took a deep breath. "Uh, nothing, never mind. Guess I'll see you tomorrow."

Turning away, she whispered, "Stupid male."

"Did you say something?"

"Nothing repeatable." She left, giving the office door just a hint of a slam.

The first council member arrived just before one.

Jason stood. "Hi, Jose. Have a seat."

Then, as others appeared, "Afternoon, gang. Bernard, Fred, Patrica, Irwin, Keith. Thanks for coming on short notice. Let's start the meeting right away. I'll try to make it quick."

Jason turned to Fred. "That electric street light you put up looks great. Can you do some more?"

"I'm making the electricity using a small steam-powered generator. It works, but it's not efficient. I've got a guy checking in Tallahassee for parts to make a larger generator that we can power with a water wheel. There's a stream, Snake Creek, you all know it, a quarter of a mile back from town. I think it would work. Thing is, the parts I need aren't free."

"Keep me informed, Fred. We'll work out something." Jason looked around the group. "There's something I need to tell the committee. Mayor Castro of Orlando wants us to either slap Susan into prison or send her back. You've seen her around. She came to Tampa a few days ago. Susan hasn't broken any rules and Castro didn't give any good reason so I've put that aside."

Bernard raised his hand. "You're making me uneasy. Mayor Castro wouldn't ask without a reason. If we ignore his request we may be sorry."

Everyone jumped as the door banged open. Tim stood in the opening, black hair wildly astray and eyes wide. He held a rifle, which he swung erratically around the room.

Jason shouted, "Tim, put that gun down! Right now!"

Tim stared at Jason, his face expressionless as if he hadn't heard, then lowered the rifle butt to the floor. White-knuckled fingers gripped the gun barrel. "May the Great Mollusk drag you all screaming into the sea! What were you council members thinking, allowing that evil thing into our town?" Lifting his rifle a few inches, he paused then opened his hand and let it fall clattering back onto the floor as he collapsed into a chair. "You're ruining my business, my income. I've got six wagons. They take fish, seafood, lots of stuff, furniture . . ."—he pointed—"furniture from your shop, Irwin. And other stuff from Tampa. My carts take it all over Florida. Anyone can see that the train you brought here is going to wipe me out. What will I do?" He lifted both hands and covered his face.

Jose stood, started to speak, paused and fingered his mustache, then said, "I've heard people say that the folks in Tallahassee are on a power grab, that they aim to boss all of Florida. Us bringing the railroad right into Tampa, aren't we inviting them in?"

Patricia's hand smacked the table. "Great Mollusk! What's wrong with you guys? We all voted in favor of the railroad. It's mighty late now for second thoughts! Sure we'll have an easy connection to the old Florida capitol. I say that's good. It's the largest town in Florida. A city, even. That's where the market is for our seafood and crafts; and it's on the way to sales opportunities further north in Old Georgia. I say we can hold our own against any bureaucrat and it won't hurt to have friends up there in case of trouble."

Jose shook his head. "I just hope the locomotive doesn't come back here pulling a car full of armed police."

Jason pushed his chair back and stood. "I have to adjourn the meeting. We'll continue discussing all this next time. You guys who are riding with me, we'll meet at the rail tracks in an hour. Have a quick lunch."

Fred tilted his chair back and then back some more. His fingers reached the door handle just as the chair feet gave a warning slip. He yanked the door open. Jason looked up to see a surprised Susan standing in the hall outside. She spun around and quickly walked away.

Jason counted the vacant stalls in the stables then turned to a woman coming towards him, her short wiry figure hardly as tall as a horse. "Hi Robin, what's happened to all the horses?"

She pushed back faded blond hair intermixed with wisps of grey. "Well Jason, seems there's a big demand for the town's horses today. I'm assuming that the riders are all out riding on official village business on this beautiful spring day."

Jason nodded. "I'm going to follow your lead, Robin, and also assume that's the case. It's best sometimes not to ask questions. Is my favorite girl available?"

"Sure is. Penny's waiting for you. Let me bring her around." She stepped away then stopped and turned back. "You just missed that new girl. What's her name?"

"Susan? Susan Smith."

"That's her. She was in a mighty big rush to saddle up and ride off. It didn't look to me like she got the surcingle properly tightened. Sure hope her saddle doesn't slip." She looked beyond Jason. "Uh oh, here come some some more of our town's exalted leaders. They'll be wanting horses, I expect."

"Yep, some of us are taking a little ride."

Robin soon returned leading Penny, already saddled. Jason mounted and flicked the reins. As Penny moved forward, Jason waived at the newcomers. He guided Penny through wide open doors and away from the stable. After a couple of hundred yards he paused in the shade of a giant live oak and sat thinking about Susan. Why was she in Tampa? Why did Orlando want her back? Did Mayor Castro really want her back or was his request designed to hide something? Jason moved Penny's reins again and rode towards the rail tracks. *There's something missing from the puzzle. Maybe just a single piece, but I have the feeling it's important.*

Jason's three companions were waiting when he arrived at the tracks. He nodded a greeting. "Irwin, Keith, Bernard, did you guys get any lunch?" Jason's stomach reminded him that he hadn't.

Keith said, "How about you, Mayor?" In response to Jason's smile and shrug Keith lifted the flap on his saddlebag and extracted something wrapped in waxed paper. "Here you are my friend, half of a peanut butter sandwich. It will keep you alive until dinner."

Jason unwrapped the offering and took a welcome bite. "Thanks." He gave Penny's neck a gentle slap. "Okay, the afternoon's passing. Let's go."

A shout. "Wait! Hold up. I'm coming with you."

They turned as Tim galloped up the path from the stable and joined the group. "Hope you don't mind, Mayor. I've been thinking about this railroad of yours and I think I can ..."

Struggling to hide his annoyance, Jason raised his hand and interrupted. "Okay, Tim. But now we have to go." His heels touched Penny's ribs and the horses started forward.

The asphalt-soaked ties between the rails troubled the horses so the group followed a sometimes indistinct path beside the tracks, veering off the path into brush when necessary. Jason contemplated the scrub forest which, as they left town, had closed in on both sides of the roadbed. Spiky palmetto, dwarf oaks and pines and unexpected gatherings of azaleas in lustrous red bloom. *I must remember to thank Robin for giving us fresh horses. They're walking well. That's good. We've got miles to go.*

A couple of hours passed, then Irwin moved alongside. "What are we looking for, Boss? Something special?"

Jason hesitated to hide momentary embarrassment. "Truthfully, I don't know. We may be wasting time, but I've been bothered by a feeling in the back of my skull that ..."

"Mayor, look!"

A figure in cream-colored trousers and shirt stepped out of the forest. Irwin said, "That's Susan!"

The horses stopped. The group sat silent as Susan pushed through waist-high brush to the railway. She stood about fifty feet ahead, facing the riders. Raising her arms she motioned for them to come closer and to bunch together. Suddenly she spun around and motioned to the trees. Immediately eight men holding rifles at their shoulders left the forest and spread apart, making a ring around Jason and the three others.

Jason raised his voice. "Susan Smith. I see that Mayor Miguel Castro tricked me. You're his spy."

She tossed her head, swirling brown hair. "Not really, Jason. Remember, I tried to warn you last night. Anyway, you should have realized that the South Florida towns would never allow you to have a railroad. That would give Tampa too much advantage. Too much power."

One of the gun-holding men stepped forward. "Too much talk. Move aside, Susan." He called to another man. "Bring the dynamite." He addressed the rest. "Keep these guys corralled. If anyone moves, even an eyebrow..."

One of the men lay down his rifle, stepped back into the shrubbery, and returned carrying a plunger box detonator, a burlap wrapped package, and a coil of wire. He freed the wires and knelt to connect them to the detonator.

The original spokesman said, "Trust me Mayor, the train isn't ever coming to Tampa again." He smiled. "And, if a few of Tampa's council members disappear along with a hunk of track, well, accidents happen."

"Wait! Stop! Stop! I can use the train!" Tim jumped from his horse and ran towards the man with the dynamite "Listen! You have to stop!" Two gunshots roared and Tim spun around and fell into the tall trackside grass.

Instantly Jason and the others snatched rifles out of their holsters, dropped from their horses to fall prone between the tracks, and fired at the surrounding attackers. Their opponents dropped into grass and brush and fired back.

Suddenly an apparition, a steam truck on rail wheels and covered with orange padding, came rushing down the rails, horn bellowing. Gun barrels protruding from the padding sent a stream of bullets into the trailside brush. The padded railcar slid to a stop, iron wheels screeching against iron track. Its protruding guns continued firing into the forest on both sides even after return shooting had stopped. Then, sudden quiet.

Jason raised his head just enough to see over the rails and then pushed up to his knees. He swung his rifle back and forth along the forest edge. Nothing moved. Tense, alert, he stood with rifle ready, then he saw a white bundle on the rails ahead. *Susan!* He ran to her, watching a red blotch spread across her cream shirt. Dropping to his knees he took her hand. "Why Susan? Why?" Green eyes looked at him for long seconds. A faint smile and her eyes closed, her hand went limp.

"Guys! Beth is hurt!" Fred was standing beside the orange padded truck. He opened the passenger door and motioned to Jason.

Jason and Keith reached the truck at the same time. Beth was slumped in the passenger seat. Blood streamed from under her hair and ran across her right cheek. Keith yanked the red bandana from around his neck and pushed it into Jason's hand. Folding it into a long strip, Jason tied it across Beth's wound. Then he held her face in both hands. "Beth, can you open your eyes?"

Her head inched up. She raised her left hand to her cheek, covering Jason's hand. Her eyes opened to look into his, her face inches from Jason's. A whisper: "Hi."

Jason smiled. "Hello, Beth. You had me scared."

"What happened?"

"It looks like a bullet got past Fred's padding and streaked across your scalp. Your face is a bloody mess, but . . ." Unintentionally, but actually intentionally, his lips moved closer to hers, touched hers and then pressed harder as hers softened in welcome.

Keith's voice. "Uh, Boss . . ."

Reluctantly Jason moved back from Beth. "What?"

"Those guys that attacked us. A couple of them are dead. Guess they ought to be buried."

Jason stood. "Yes, help me drag the bodies into the bushes. Soon as we get back I'll send a team to do the burying."

Keith hesitated. "Uh, the girl, too?"

Jason stood silent, looking at the red-stained, cream-colored bundle lying on the ties. "Susan made a choice. She was one of them. She doesn't deserve any better or worse than the others. We'll bury her body with her friends."

They both jumped as Tim suddenly rose up from a bush. He gripped one arm with a bloody hand. "Somebody bandage my arm!" He faced Jason. "Those idiots wanted to destroy my new business! I can use the train after all. My carts will be loaded here and put on the train. At the other end I'll have horses to pull the carts to my customers. Faster service and less cost."

Jason nodded. "Sounds good, Irwin, everyone wins." He turned to find Fred standing at his side. "Fred, your new creation, whatever the heck it is, that's your best invention yet."

Fred looked at the ground. He rubbed his chin. He dug at the dirt with the toe of his boot. "Sorry about the orange padding. It's the only color the Tallahassee scrap yard had."

"Don't be sorry. Your orange monster rushing down the tracks with its horn blaring spooked our attackers, helped scare them off. Specially with you and Beth shooting like crazy. You two saved our lives." He raised his voice. "Hey guys! Let's grab the loose horses and head back."

A soft hand grasped his. "I'm going back with you."

"No way, Beth. You're a walking wounded. I won't let you ride horseback. You're going back to Tampa in Fred's contraption."

"Jason." Her eyes fixed on his.

He sighed. "Okay. You take the saddle. I'll sit behind you. I'll be holding your waist tight so you won't fall off."

She smiled. "I think that will be just fine."

Sea Jackals of Dubai

by Mark Mellon

A FAIR WIND BLEW FROM SHORE the early morning *Efreet* set forth with the tide on another long voyage.

"Set the mainsail full, Orhansik. Keep her close to the wind," Jilderiz ordered.

"Aye, Kaptan," the mate replied.

Orhansik barked orders. Hands grasped lines and heaved. The dirty, hempen lateen sail creaked aloft and billowed as it caught the wind. *Efreet* steadily made way, slicing through whitecaps. Low on the horizon, a reddish gold sun broke through gray clouds and shone on the long, black ship and the green banner hung from her topmast. Gathered on the pier to bid farewell and godspeed, families and friends exulted at the good omen. Men fired rifles and women joyously ululated. Syndjad watched everything he ever knew slowly recede, green mountains, his family, his mother.

"You aren't sad, Syndjad? I hope you don't regret your decision."

"Oh, no, Uncle—I mean, Kaptan."

Jilderiz chuckled and twirled his long mustachio.

"Get below. Help Bakhtab. First watch will want breakfast soon."

Syndjad went below to the tiny, hot galley. Pot-bellied Bakhtab labored over a hot sea stove.

"About time. Fetch water."

Bakhtab cooked wheat cakes. On the first day out, the crew would have honey with them.

"Open a barrel of figs. First watch is always hungry."

"How long will it take to reach Dubai?"

"When we return, you'll have a beard. Get the trays ready."

First watch was piped to breakfast at five bells. Syndjad received good natured

71

jibes as he served them.

"Watch out, boy. There's evil spirits in Dubai. Men with faces in their stomachs who eat boys."

"The Kaptan told me about those tales. I know what's in Dubai."

"And what would that be?" another hand asked.

"Why, treasure, of course."

"Aye, lad, but only if you've the nerve to take it," Bakhtab said.

Jilderiz ordered the mainsail reefed and fished once *Efreet* cleared the Bar Al-Weddell's vast expanse.

"Fire the engine, Orhansik."

The mate went below. A rumble shook the wooden ship down to her keelson. Black smoke poured from the cylindrical bronze stack. The bow screw turned. A methane fueled engine drove the ship at increasing speed. *Efreet*'s narrow keel sliced effortlessly through endless gray green waters. The intricately carved, female demon figurehead screeched fiercely at the waves to make way. *Efreet* was the only ship, a lone voyager.

The crew quickly settled down to the steady routine of life at sea. *Efreet* traveled at fifteen knots an hour through churning, ever restless seas. When the wind blew strongly in the right direction, miserly Jilderiz had the sail hoisted to save fuel. Jilderiz closely checked his compass and ancient, spring-driven watches. Every day, precisely at noon, he or Orhansik stood on the foredeck and took a sighting with a gleaming bronze sextant, a centuries old artifact, the Aluwassi clan's most treasured possession.

Syndjad soon mastered his duties. He wanted to be an able bodied sailor. He learned not only to help Bakhtab cook, but the ship's intricate network of lines and the many, difficult knots used to secure them so he could help the crew hand and reef. Soon he scampered up ratlines fast as any other hand. Jilderiz taught him the intricate art of navigation and Orhansik gave grumpy lessons in the maintenance and operation of the engine, an object of veneration and tender care to the crew. After several weeks, confident he knew all there was to sailing, Syndjad mostly overlooked his primal fear of the endless, roiling waters with never a hint of land.

Then *Efreet* hit the roaring forties. Never calm, the sea now raged, throwing up towering waves that brutally smashed into the bows to douse the deck with briny water. *Efreet* fought up steep crests, only to slide down each time into a deep trough with yet another foam-crested wall of water headed directly toward her. Despite oil-skins, every man was drenched. The engine doggedly pushed the ship ahead, but Orhansik argued with Jizderil about fuel. Unable to take sightings, they navigated by dead reckoning alone and trusted to God and the sea's emptiness to spare them from deadly shoals or a lee shore's perils. Captain and mate alternated watches on the poop, Jilderiz on night watches.

One night Syndjad stood with Jilderiz as an unbelievable volume of rain smashed down. Treacherous cross-currents hurtled waves toward the ship from all directions. Syndjad could see no further than his hand before his face.

"Orhansik will kill us all. Curse his mother's organ. Go below, boy, and tell him more speed."

"Aye, sir."

He grabbed a lifeline and went hand over hand to the forward hatchway, fast as he could in the face of implacable rain. Syndjad held onto the lifeline with one hand and bent low to lift the hatch. A wave leapt over the port gunwale and smashed into him. Feet swept away, Syndjad slid helplessly, about to be go overboard. Strong as an iron vise, a hand clamped onto his right ankle and yanked him below into the hold. He hit the ladder hard and gasped, banged up, but alive. Orhansik was indistinct in the hold's murky light.

"What is it, boy?"

"Kaptan says more speed, sir."

Orhansik grunted.

"Can't. Kaptan was a fool to send you. Stay below."

Efreet rode out that terrible night and many more. Jilderiz and his men endured, sailed on. The roaring forties slowly slipped past. Gradually, the winds stilled, the skies cleared, and the crew cheered when the sun reappeared. For the first time in days, Jilderiz took a sighting at noon and consulted the charts in his cabin. He emerged on deck fairly content to the crew's relief. Bakhtab had Syndjad troll for fish with a baited, hooked line. He pulled in rays and skates. The hands gratefully ate grilled flesh.

In the crow's nest at dawn, high atop the waving mast, delighted by the bright red sun's appearance, Syndjad closely scanned the horizon. *Efreet* forged ahead, black smoke plumes trailing behind. A small, hazy red line appeared due north. Startled, Syndjad rubbed his eyes and looked hard again. The smudge was growing larger.

"Land ho! The Hot Lands!"

He grabbed a backstay and slid down to the deck.

"The Hot Lands! Just ahead!"

He was surprised and ashamed when the hands burst into laughter.

"Silly lubber," Bakhtab said. "We're nowhere near. That's just Al-Afreek's southern tip. We've still many leagues to cross."

"Don't mock him," Orhansik said. "He's a willing hand. Get aloft again and keep a close watch, Syndjad."

"Aye, sir."

An experienced Kaptan with over two dozen voyages, Jilderiz set a course for a deep bay at the continent's southeastern tip. Syndjad saw his first ruins, an ancient lighthouse's jagged trunk, shattered stones and crumbled concrete, pitiful wrecks of what were once proud, imperial buildings.

"What was this place called?"

"It doesn't matter," Jilderiz answered. "They were sinners. God punished them. They deserve to be forgotten."

Efreet anchored near shore. The hands lowered the launch and jolly boat. They harvested kelp that grew close to shore—fed oxygen by fresh water that trickled from depleted rivers—and also thin, yellow, seasonal grass that grew on otherwise bare hills. The vegetation was crammed into the engine's ravenous maw, packed in tight with even more set aside by Orhansik in the hold in bales, enough raw fuel to hopefully last the voyage's next leg. Bakhtab and Syndjad went through the ruins with large burlap bags, hunting for buried, preserved wood for the cook fire. There was no life other than buzzing, blue-winged insects that fed off the grass. Bakhtab wiped the sweat from his brow.

Engine refueled and water casks full, *Efreet* left the bay and set her course north. Al-Afreek's shoreline stretched out to port, the edge of a continent far larger than Al-Antart, but ravaged, devoid of growth, only bare, dun hills and occasional ruins, tumbledown heaps of stone bleached skull white by acidic rain. The ship passed through a broad strait between Al-Afreek and a large island, stripped bare to the rock. Jizderil pointed to the island's dead carcass.

"The Bones of Mudahshqir. Once it was a green and flourishing place, or so legend says. We're about halfway to Dubai. So far you've done well. Keep it up, lad."

Efreet continued into an ocean. With each day the temperature steadily rose until Syndjad thought he would collapse.

"Take your time, boy," Bakhtab said. "Drink from the scuttlebutt and keep to the shade. The Hot Lands you wanted to see? We're getting closer. But this heat is nothing compared to what's to come."

Efreet sailed past the Alkarn Aleezem, the Great Horn, and into red waters. There was the engine's steady rattle, the wind's rustle through the lines, but otherwise silence. Jilderiz smiled broadly. Even Orhansik seemed relatively cheerful.

"How far now, Bakhtab?"

"To the Kalee Al-Arab and Dubai? Perhaps a hundred leagues, probably more. Get wood."

Efreet sailed swiftly. After three days, a hand called, "Land ho!"

The fabled Al-Arab lay in the distance, a shimmering, yellow ochre smear, ancient homeland of the Aluwassi. They made port at Soqqot, an island where, although reduced to a dribble, a fresh-water spring still supported enough thin greenery to let the crew refuel and rewater. Jizderil drove the crew hard, determined to stay on schedule, keenly aware of winter's short span.

They approached the Rasool Jabal shortly after six bells of the morning watch. Once the narrow inlet to the world's shallowest gulf, the Madek Harmoz had considerably broadened and deepened. To round the strait's curve and enter the Kalee Al-Arab was still no easy navigational feat though. The waters were studded with shipwrecks and mines from long ago wars, some still able to seek out and destroy a ship.

"The wind blows from the east, Orhansik. Raise the sail."

Sail set at a cross angle to the strong wind, *Efreet* tacked round the cape.

"You made it, boy. The Kalee. Climb the mast. See if you spy Dubai."

Syndjad hurried up the ratlines to the crow's nest. To starboard a hazy shore wavered, former home of the long extinct Farsis. He kept his eyes to port, closely scanned the landscape as it passed. As with Al-Afreek, shattered ruins fringed the shore, but nothing substantial. Patient after long watches at sea, Syndjad kept watch. Heat lulled him, sapped his strength and made him drowsy. He fought off lethargy, shaded his eyes with his hands, and looked forward.

There. Was it just sun on the water playing tricks with his eyes? No. Definitely there. Sunlight reflected in a blinding gleam, the kind of light only glass gave off.

"The Hutam Safina! I see it!"

"Where away?" Jizderil shouted.

"Three points off the port bow."

Jizderil ordered the course adjusted. *Efreet* steamed southwest. The light grew more distinct as the noon sun blazed down. A gray blur in the distance grew from indistinct smears on a wavering shoreline into definite shapes. Once mighty and modern, a city lay destroyed amid shallow waters. Foremost among the ruins, outthrust into the gulf, stood a gray stump that once gleamed blinding white, ragged, battered top long ago shorn of its curved crest. A few intact panes in the remaining stories reflected the sun, the light that caught Syndjad's eye. The Hutam Safina, the Shipwreck.

Gargantuan piles of rubble littered the shallows, heaps of concrete, glass, and steel, millions of tons of wreckage only millennia would ultimately erase. Two piles were bigger than the others, tall as Al-Antart mountains. No bird cried or fouled the ruins with waste. There was no insect hum, no animal cries from shore, only Orhansik's shouted commands as the engine shut down and the hands dropped anchors.

"Now we really earn our salt," Jizderil said.

Syndjad learned the hard truth of these words in the days to come. Jilderiz drove the crew without letup, determined to obtain as much cargo as possible while weather permitted. Hands rose well before dawn to eat, wash, and say prayers at dawn's first glint, bowed in the direction of the Forbidden Cities. Aside from breaks for prayer and food, every waking moment was devoted to scavenging. Details went out in the launch and jolly boat with strict orders not to return without valuable goods.

To search the ruins was hard and dangerous work. Broken glass and rusty, razor sharp metal was everywhere. Hands dug with picks and shovels to wrest treasure from the rubble. They sank shafts into large heaps that sometimes collapsed. Men were pulled out by ropes tied around their waists as they spat out dirt and gasped for air.

They looked for precious metals, platinum, silver, gold, copper, and titanium steel, substances otherwise unobtainable in Al-Antart. Jewels were valued as well, but mostly as gifts. Most treasured of all was any artifact from the Aljann, the Paradise Time, a scientific instrument such as a compass or binoculars or, best of all, a book, rarest and most precious pearl, a literal storehouse of knowledge. In addition to the jolly boat and the launch, the ship's smith fashioned small, shallow draft boats from aluminum wreckage. Two man crews went out to find quick, easy pickings in smaller rubble heaps.

"Good thing you're with me," Bakhtab puffed as he rowed. "I know the best places."

The heat was miserable, the sky overcast with gray, pink-edged clouds. They rowed past battered concrete pillars crowned with twisted, rusty rebar.

"Are you sure we'll find anything? Most of the men dig in the Boorj."

Bakhtab snorted. "So rocks can fall on us? I took enough risks just getting here. I know to steer clear of the Boorj and the other big heap too. Believe me, even a small pile has good pickings. There was never a treasure trove like Dubai, not unless some djinn guards it."

Bakhtab steered for a low slung building at the ruins' edge, near the Hutam Safina. Two stories above the waterline were still intact.

"See that sign, boy?"

Faded, red consonant swirls on a wall read *Matjar Majwaharat*. Jewelry Store.

"See how easy it is? Tie the boat off here."

Shallow, hot water reached Syndjad's waist. They clambered up a staircase's shattered remains. Bakhtab battered down the remnants of a door with his club and peered inside.

"Doesn't look like anyone's been here. Let's go inside."

The long, white room was encrusted with dust, piled so high it was impossible to see inside the glass display cases. Bakhtab and Syndjad carefully lifted off the tops. Jadestones, emeralds, diamonds, and pearls were mixed with heavy red, gold, and silver necklaces, bracelets, and rings. Bakhtab rifled through the jewelry.

"Stick to metals. Fill your bag with them, especially platinum and gold. Take a few jewels for your mother and sweetheart if you like, but otherwise business first."

"What's this?"

"Why, it's a sort of magnifying glass. Keep that as a present for the Kaptan."

Syndjad tucked the artifact under his headband for safekeeping. There was a noise outside, something hitting metal.

"Quick," Bakhtab hissed. "The floor."

They hit the floor. Male voices broke the silence, unfamiliar ones in a strange dialect. Bakhtab motioned for Syndjad to follow. They crawled to the wall and peered down through a window. Men were below, swathed from head to foot in gray rags, astride long-legged, hump-backed animals of a kind Syndjad had never seen before. Each man had a long, curved sword in a sheath and a long-barreled rifle slung over his back.

"Ajanib," Bakhtab murmured. "I'd heard tales of barbarians, but never believed them until now. What an ill looking bunch."

"What shall we do?"

"You'll go back and warn the Kaptan."

"Swim back?"

Bakhtab nodded. "It's foul water with bad ruins in the bargain. But you're young and strong and you've got your boots on. Go on, sneak out back."

"But what about you, Bakhtab?"

"I'm too old and fat. Besides, someone has to distract them. And this should do it."

Bakhtab lovingly caressed his club.

"Now go while you can, but stay down."

Syndjad shot Bakhtab a pleading look, but his stern, silent response bid him to his duty. He crawled across the floor to a window on the opposite wall and looked out. The water was deeper on this side. He hung onto the window ledge and lowered himself feet first. Syndjad swam to a nearby rubble heap where he hid on the opposite side.

There were shouts from the building in the foreign dialect, then silence punctuated by a surprised, anguished scream. More shouts followed by a horrible, guttural gasp from Bakhtab, run through by swords as he fought to the last.

"Motherless scum. God curse them."

Syndjad almost gave way to tears until he remembered he was a sailor under orders, with a mission to perform. He carefully weighed his options. If he picked his way through the ruins back to *Efreet*, the Ajanib might catch him or he could injure himself on sharp rocks or broken glass. On the other hand, if he swam away from the ruins into open water and headed toward *Efreet*, that would be the fastest way to reach her. The Ajanib were obvious lubbers and couldn't catch him that way.

Syndjad waded in until the water was chest deep and pushed off. He kept his head high while he breaststroked. The water was calm, but it wasn't long before it began to eat at him. Mild itching slowly grew into distinct discomfort that built from there into flaming agony. As Bakhtab bid him, his boots were still on so they gave some protection, heavy drag that they were, but his bare hands felt as if they were about to dissolve in pure bleach.

Efreet was visible, a long, narrow, black silhouette. Yet the more he swam, the increasingly more distant the ship seemed. Syndjad tried to stay calm, to keep his breath even and his strokes measured, but the irrational will to survive at all costs escalated to panic.

He fought just to keep his head above water, kicked his legs and cursed the heavy boots, and was about to go under when powerful hands reached down, grabbed him by the shoulders, and hauled him into the launch.

"What were you about, boy?"

Syndjad coughed and gasped.

"Ajanib, sir. Bakhtab and I saw them. He sent me back to give warning."

Orhansik nodded.

"Row for the ship, smartly."

The launch fairly shot back to *Efreet*. Orhansik was first over the side with Syndjad behind him.

"He and Bakhtab have seen Ajanib, Kaptan. Bakhtab sent Syndjad to report."

"And what happened to Bakhtab?"

"The Ajanib killed him, Kaptan. I heard them while I was hiding."

Jizderil's face grew red. He pulled hard on his mustachio.

"Orhansik."

"Yes, Kaptan?"

"Up steam."

The crew stared dumbfounded at Jilderiz. Bakhtab murdered and his only response was to turn tail and run? Even zealous Orhansik seemed unhappy. Still, *Efreet* was a taut ship and the crew obeyed orders. The ship headed away from Dubai, toward the Rasool Kabal. Syndjad was taken below and rubbed with grease to salve his burned skin. When twilight came, Jizderil ordered Orhansik to the quarter deck.

"Down steam. Raise the sail and put the ship about."

"So we're going back to Dubai?" Orhansik said, startled from taciturnity.

"Of course. Do you think I'll just let barbarians kill my cook? He was with me for a dozen voyages. I only sailed away to deceive them. Those intruders from the Zagros will die like the villains they are."

Efreet sailed silently through darkness, ropes and tackle greased to prevent creaks. It was four bells after the first watch when the sail was reefed and fished. *Efreet* slowly lost way and came to a halt just outside the ruins. The crew formed up for a raiding party.

"What are you doing here, boy? You're in sick bay."

"Please, mate, let me go. I'm fit for duty."

"Let him go, Orhansik. He has a shipmate to avenge."

The crew got into the jolly boat and launch with a few hands left behind to guard the ship. Muffled oars on greased tholes glided noiselessly through the water. Every man kept absolute silence, under strict orders to not even sneeze. They rowed through ruins in darkness. Jizderil stood in the launch's prow, eyes and ears open, and relied on his expert knowledge of Dubai. The boats slowly approached the few places where there was sufficient dry land to let a large body of men and animals camp. After an hour, there was no sign of them. Despair welled up inside Syndjad. The cowards had fled.

Jizderil held up his right hand. Instantly, oars on both boats tossed up in one smooth, noiseless motion. They lost way. Jizderil sniffed. Syndjad smelled it too, smoke. Every man tensed at the prospect of imminent action. Jizderil signaled for Orhansik to maneuver the jolly boat to the camp's opposite side. Once the boat left, he waited fifteen minutes by his watch and then waved his hand forward. The oars fell. The launch gained way.

"Easy now," Jizderil hissed.

They drew close to the camp, blocked from view by ruins and darkness. The smoke smell was strong, with red glints occasionally visible through gaps in the walls. There were loud voices and a sharp, animal bawl. Jizderil signaled for the hands to disembark. The water stung his legs, but Syndjad pushed ahead with the others, careful to make no noise as he did.

They crouched behind a crumbled wall. The camp lay just beyond. Syndjad peeped over the wall. There were cook fires with a circle of men around each one. A watch was kept, but they kept close to the fires and were inattentive. The beasts were in an enclosure fashioned from scrap metal. The reek from the pen was horrible. The hand nearest Syndjad yanked him down.

"Don't give us away, boy," Jizderil whispered. "At my signal, stand and fire a volley. Then we charge."

Jizderil held his arm high and brought it down. With tolerable uniformity, the hands stood, leveled their rifles, and fired them at near point blank range into the Ajanib's camp. Men keeled over, shot in the back. The beasts went wild. They screamed and hurled themselves at the enclosure, tore themselves wide open in desperate attempts to escape. There was an answering volley from the opposite side. Orhansik and his men.

"Come on then."

Jilderiz and his men charged. Syndjad pulled his sword and followed. They laid into the remaining Ajanib, ignored plaintive cries for mercy as they hacked them to pieces. A man pointed his rifle at Syndjad, but the weapon misfired. Syndjad ran to him and drove his sword through the man's stomach. Some hands badly cut themselves in their frenzy to murder the Ajanib. Orhansik and his party ran up and joined in the slaughter. All were massacred. Jilderiz held his arms high.

"Centuries ago, God decreed the Aluwassi alone may harvest the riches of

Dubai. Death to any barbarian who dares to intrude."

The bodies were stripped of their rags to be used for fuel. Naked corpses were left to rot. Several beasts were shot to salt their meat for the return voyage, the rest driven into the ruins to starve. The next day, dark pillars of cloud loomed over the empty desert, far off in the interior, harbingers of the deadly simooms. Hold full of treasure, *Efreet* upped steam and set course northeast. A long voyage back lay ahead, but the ship was sturdy and the crew seasoned and brave.

And of all the hands who sailed her, none did so with a gladder heart than Syn-djad. For he was an Aluwassi, a son of the sea, destined to sail her waters as his ancestors had, as God had long ago decreed.

The following is the conclusion of Violet Bertelsen's novella *The Ghosts in Little Deer's Grove*.

"Part One: Hither and Thither" was published in *Into the Ruins: Spring 2019* (Issue #12), which can be found at intotheruins.com or at your local or online book seller.

THE GHOSTS IN LITTLE DEER'S GROVE

PART TWO: WHENCE AND WHITHER

BY VIOLET BERTELSEN

CHAPTER 1: THE THREADS OF MEMORY

Nitzah

A LITTLE AFTER I WAS BORN THE UNIVERSITIES WENT OUT OF BUSINESS. Before this, the Pioneer Valley was then known as a center of higher education. Over three fatal months while I was three the economy came crashing down, and after a few terrible months there was the beginning of the five long years of Civil War. During this time, the colleges were mostly shut down and never reopened. The region's major source of income came from the students spending their future earnings to attend, what was in essence, adult day care. It sounds unbelievable today, but it is true; an entire generation couldn't afford to have children because of the debts they accrued trying to get educated.

That sort of perverse arrangement can only last so long, and around the age of three my parents' world came crashing down. My father was a weak-willed professor and he succumbed to too much drink and too weak of a liver when I was seven, only a year from the ceasefire agreement. My mama, who was still attractive, managed to marry Henry, a younger red-headed farmer of quiet temperament and endless toil. Mama was an herbalist by trade and taught me her arts.

This may be hard to understand about our time, but it is true; there were many men who yearned to be able to turn into women and women who wished to become men. At the age of fifteen I paid a local veterinarian to castrate me. Afterwards, I took the name Nitzah from a vision and mama accepted me as her daughter. Everyday I took female herbal remedies and birth control pills while they were still easy to get, and I grew little breasts. No one cared very much; life is crazy and people are strange. A little after this I befriended Oliver, who was about twelve and tough as nails. He had been orphaned from the Civil War a decade ago. After his aunt died of a drug overdose, he had lived on the street, surviving through his wits. Oliver was interested in herbs, and after we met at a calamus patch I began teaching him all that I knew. We met several times a week until the fighting broke out.

The valley was able to slowly adjust itself to making do with the excellent alluvial soils that abounded. We were fortunate to be close enough to the Connecticut river to sell bulk goods to the merchants who gathered in Holyoke, one of the richest river towns with its beautiful canals and old brickwork. With enough time anything can become normal.

Life is unpredictable, strange and completely baffling. Growing up, things were bad, but then for a while they seemed to settle down. There had been some fighting in the south and west and big parts of the country had partitioned off, but we were still part of the twenty-two states left of the old USA. There was some fear that Canadian forces might break our feeble defenses in Maine. Canada now was a resource-cursed nation where most people worked in the mines supplying China with her trickle of raw materials. Miners were especially feared in speculations of war, having the reputation as the deadliest soldiers.

The old United States had maintained enough of its power and bristling don't-tread-on-me stance to keep up a certain parity with China and Russia and Brazil, the new world powers. It did this, however, on the terms of surrender. We had to cut off huge sections of the country to maintain whatever independence we still had. The states of the old Confederacy began to be administered by Brazil. Russia set up barons in Alaska and all the way down the coast to Sebastopol, California where Russian became the official language and most people were forced into becoming tenant farmers. China managed to draw the western half of the country into her sphere, from Los Angeles to Kansas City, including Hawaii of course. Texas took Oklahoma and most of New Mexico and become its own country. It seemed obvious from the outside that the presidents of Texas were little more than the paid puppets of Mexico City.

The twenty-two Northeastern states had banded together to try to hold out against this new and hostile balance of world power. This arrangement lasted until I was about twenty-four and then the Revolutionaries began agitating for a new order.

I remember: Andy and Rosa had guns. My only arms were a bow and arrow I took off a dead kid we found by some little creek. He seemed to have died of hunger; he wasn't a good hunter. In his tent were some matches, a bow and a quiver of five arrows. Since Andy and Rosa had guns they decided that I should carry the bow and arrows. "It's better than nothing," said Andy entirely without humor.

We must have been carrying medical supplies, tinctures and clean bandages. There was probably a lot of ephedra tincture so the troops would be able to fight for days without sleep. This was equally good for siege warfare and for defending against a siege. We had repulsed some of the Constitutionalists from strongholds by employing ephedra. Our position had been the weaker and yet we had triumphed. The blitzkrieg idea had been mine, but Andy had taken credit for it, much to my relief. For that reason, he carried a gun seriously, while I was still trying to figure out if there might be a way to escape other than suicide. In my jacket, I carried a two-ounce bottle of poison hemlock tincture at all times, just in case. I hated the Revolutionaries and found myself trapped in the worst sort of bitter metallic tasting irony being pressed into their service. My mama had always taught me to be a Constitutionalist and conservative.

We walked through the light dust of snow, the sky gray and overcast. The temperature was just below freezing. We walked in good spirits feeling light and easy, well-fed and well-rested, not imagining that we were about to step into open enemy fire, which is exactly what happened. Since I was a medic and was clearly not the most loyal to the Revolution, I had no gun, just the bow, the quiver, a pocket knife, and steel toed boots as my weapons. Andy had a gun slung over his shoulders and was carrying Molotov cocktails in a wooden box. I don't remember why; when I died I was very stoned, so stoned that I still find it hard to recall all the details hundreds of years later.

Rosa had an excellent repeating deer hunting rifle. The whole gun thing always turned me off. I didn't want to deal with the responsibility that carrying such a tool entailed.

Bullets began to whiz around our heads. There was no solid cover, just these regularly spaced Douglas fir trees. It must have been an abandoned Christmas tree farm. We ran and took cover behind trees, running in three different zigzag patterns, like bounding deer. After about half a minute the shooting tapered off. Andy whipped two Molotov cocktails as he ran from his position. With that, both Rosa and I took flight too, she giving covering fire.

Two of the trees burst into flames, and one man began screaming trying to stop the fire that was all over his body. In less than a minute he passed out. We used this distraction to retreat further, trying to get back to our stronghold. As we zigzagged back, bullets whizzed by us and one grazed my ribcage, burning it, hardly drawing blood.

‡‡

When we returned to the camp in the farmhouse we learned that we had been under friendly fire. Luckily for us we had been under the command of the Sergeant Major. The platoon we had repulsed had been following orders of an arrogant and stupid staff Sergeant. Ultimately he faced the firing squad for that or some other insubordination; I don't remember the exact details.

Sergeant Major was impressed with our gallantry and our ability to outmaneuver a superior force. He was especially interested in Andy and Rose's tight, spontaneous technique. "If we had medals, you would all receive them, even you Nitzah," he said. "You would receive a purple heart."

When the revolutionary force found our house and I had somehow managed to talk the bored and nervous teenagers into letting us live, events had gotten increasingly strange. Andy suggested that we throw a party; the troops and everyone else went on a three-day bender where at least seventy percent of my tinctures were swallowed as booze. The conversations were difficult for me to follow. Instead of playing the sorts of games that I prefer—such as "cool plants," "dancing," or "let's make it ourselves!"—they played games like "body count," where they'd all try to figure out exactly the number of people they had killed; "bullet wounds," where they bragged about their scars; and "arson," where they recounted the tales of improbably large fires. I listened and did my best to weigh in with stories of animal butchering gone wrong and recalling epically nasty wounds I had healed with herbs. The soldiers were impressed. They took us back with them, not as prisoners, but as recruits thanks to Rosa's in-depth understanding of their doctrine, Andy's ability to play along, and the obvious fact that I was a skilled herbalist who could function adroitly as a medic using common weeds.

Equal to how much I hated the troops of the Revolutionary army, I loved our Sergeant Major. He was the commanding officer, and was everything that the Revolutionary Army wasn't: intelligent, circumspect, polite and curious. Sergeant Major struck me as an excellent judge of character. He was able to always maintain a certain degree of remoteness from the antics of his battalion. His mannerisms were decidedly blue collar, and he once shared with me that he had been a mechanic before all of this started. It was clear from talking with him that he had read a lot of books very deeply in his free time.

Immediately he took a certain liking to me. Having pondered this for several hundred years, I believe that what he liked most about me is that I hated the revolution with every fiber of my being. He was surrounded by sycophants and toadies who had decided to confer him the status of a Great Man given his brilliant success at the Battle of Northampton. He found me fun and naughty, like a cat. Whenever he had the chance he would lure me into telling him about herbs. We did so about six times.

One time in particular I remember clearly even now. The Sergeant had congested mucus and a bad cough. I made him thyme infusion with honey, which helped almost immediately. As he drank the tea slowly, he asked me to explain my differential diagnoses of coughs, why I had selected thyme, and my thoughts on vulneraries to lure me into talking more deeply of herb craft. As he was my commanding officer, I was compelled to follow orders, and even though I enjoyed talking with him, the power imbalance always struck me as embarrassingly arbitrary and awkward for honest exchange.

"Well sir, with thyme what I value most is what Nicholas Culpeper wrote in the 1600s, saying that it is a 'noble strengthener of the lungs.' I find it perhaps the most generally useful herb for congestive respiratory issues, especially when there is some evidence of hard dried mucus. Thyme dissolves this stagnancy. It works on both the upper and lower respiratory system. Since there are so many 'pipes and passageways' of the lungs, thyme helps when mucus has begun to obstruct breathing. I use it in less serious cases, such as yours, sir. If there was a lot of green adhesive mucus, I'd use pine and if there was great excess of mucus I'd use elecampane. For dry coughs I'd use a mallow or violet leaf. Mullein I'd reserve to a deep dry cough that hurt the ribs. If there were a chronic cough that always sounded like clearing the throat I'd suggest wild cherry bark, and if there were a sore throat in the picture I'd give an infusion of sage leaf honey and a little vinegar. Garlic can be good too, probably it is the most universal remedy we have and I think it is best as a preventative taken daily. It helps build up the body's defenses."

"Duly noted," he responded, leaning against a large grey rock.

"And with first aid herbs, Culpeper always was helpful in furthering my understanding; he suggested yarrow for hemorrhage, Solomon's seal for broken bones to knit them back together, and St. John's Wort and goldenrod as singularly good. He also explored this herb," I said, pointing to the ground.

"Plantain," said the Sergeant Major, half smiling. "*Plantago major.*"

"Yes sir, exactly, he found it also singularly good for all sorts of wounds, new and old, and it is unparalleled at pulling out pus, dirt and venom from a wound. When there isn't a vent to pull out infection I employ calendula which helps to drain the wound from the inside. St John's Wort is better for extremely painful wounds and puncture-wounds and prevents tetanus. To this excellent little platoon of vulnery herbs, I add cayenne as a more powerful and general hemostatic, an agent that stops bleeding, and of course as I have proven time and time again the value raw wildflower honey has for aiding healing. I think that it does its best work when let to sit over calendula or St. John's Wort flowers, but it is also mighty fine on its own."

He nodded, taking it all in. He didn't speak for a moment, appearing to me far away and deep in thought. "Growing up I loved Kipling. That was a long time ago. I read all of his work, that and all the work of Tolkien, C.S. Lewis and Jack London. Kipling has an excellent story about Nicholas Culpeper; I wish I had my full library here, I'd let you read it. Here books tend to turn into kindling or toilet paper . . ." He coughed and took the last swig of his thyme tea. "Thank you, Nitzah; since we promoted you to Medic your techniques have saved dozens of men's lives and limbs. It is a lot of information to take in, and I doubt I'll be able to master it, but I appreciate your work with us. It is life-saving; with your understanding of plants you can do things that the Revolutionary MDs cannot." Maybe he said more or less, it's hard to remember every detail.

"Thank you, sir!" I stammered, blushing. He dismissed me with orders to gather vulnerary herbs. As I left, I saw him collapse on to his cot, utterly exhausted.

CHAPTER TWO: LOVE AND WAR

Sergeant Major

They were an odd bunch for sure. Most of our fighting force were laboring men: farmers, mechanics, machinists, miners. I came from a long line of mechanics. Before the hostilities erupted, what would become the Revolutionary Army had been a bunch of disparate groups with many disparate ideas. Some believed in capitalism, others national socialism, some libertarianism, others fascism. The one thing they had in common is they drove pickup trucks and were very angry.

They had seen their jobs turn to shit and their friends die of opiates peddled by doctors and their own dreams and aspirations weaponized against them. The young men in my charge however were mostly bewildered. They mouthed our slogans but their hearts weren't in it, and when they were it was with the humorlessness of a brainwashed fanatic.

The truth was that our revolution had didn't have a coherent ideology, instead we had a lot of anger and hate that was channeled into fighting. We also were, by and large, of a certain class that was getting taxed really hard by the old United States. Increasingly, people didn't deal in money much at all, and instead relied on informal exchanges to get by. We, on the other hand, had to deal in money to put gas in the trucks we needed to haul our tools, and that money got taken by the government. We aimed to attract as many people as possible to the cause, and a very general philosophy was established. Traditionalism was the main commonality. The idea of a glorious past we could force other people to create. It was always a bad idea, and we would see so too with our own eyes soon enough.

The counterpart of our glorious imagined Traditionalism was degeneracy. It was everything evil that we wanted to destroy. We hated the United States Government but we despised degeneracy and vowed to purge it from our lands by point of sword. We never actually defined degeneracy coherently or set upon a plan of how to purge it. It simply was a word that meant "I hate you," and little else.

Some took a mystical approach and urged the path of cleansing oneself of personal degeneracy to lead a more upstanding life. Others wanted to torture and kill degenerates and utterly obliterate them. This was less popular than you'd expect. Our Generalissimo himself called this bloodthirsty and demonic attitude "degenerate sadism" and it was officially discouraged. Mostly people didn't really care about the cause; they just knew that they'd be shot if they deserted. The young men weren't difficult to control. Most preferred their life as a well-fed soldier fighting for sovereignty to that of a peasant struggling to stave off hunger.

This may sound absolutely insane, and it certainly was. We were only able to do as much as we did because we were receiving a lot of arms and bars of sterling silver from the Chinese government, which was pretty clearly trying to further partition the old United States into quarrelling countries they could better exploit. Their hand was stronger than ours ultimately, but at the time that Nitzah, Andy and Rosa joined our ranks, we were flush with victory and there was a palpable euphoria as we took more and more territory.

When they marched into camp dressed as soldiers I interviewed them, learned their skills and pondered how to use them. They all had uneven haircuts and a lot of tattoos. Soon I learned that they were all in an agonizing love triangle. Andy and Nitzah wanted to keep on with their homosexual love affair, and Nitzah was smart enough to get what he wanted.

Nitzah was a striking person. He was this very effeminate castrated homosexual, who wore dresses and pretended to be a woman. Upon our first visit he cut the bullshit: "Sir, please look," he said, looking at me the way a beautiful woman sizes up a suitor. "I am an herbalist and I have practiced for six years on my own. I know how to heal wounds, and have cured countless sick people. I am skilled in the medicines of hill and stream and tree. I know the plants inside and out, and can use this knowledge to your ends. I can do things your best doctors can't because nature is my pharmacy." He was telling the truth too, and he did save countless lives.

His healing abilities were excellent. Not only the hard skills of diagnoses and treatment, but also the softer skills of nursing, of comforting. He was skilled at becoming a mother, and once explained to me, in detail, why mothering was so important. "Sir, have you read Desmond Morris' *Naked Ape*?"

"Hmmm, no."

"Well sir, it discusses how many people get sick just so they can receive a parent's touch or medical equivalent from a nurse or doctor. I don't have the book on hand but he made a very persuasive point and even cites numerous studies. So I make sure anyone who I tend gets a clinical healing touch. It is my job to help the Revolutionary Army win, sir, and it matters little if it is the touch or the tea that gets your men fighting again. The methodology is pointless to examine to a certain extent, sir, since what matters, in war, are the results."

He was able to size me up just as cannily as I measured him. Nitzah understood that I was in a position where results were much more important than theory and because of that, the more powerful he made himself, the better go of it he'd have in the Revolutionary Army. He was, after all, pretty much the definition of a degenerate.

Andy and Rosa, who to a great extent hated each other, were much better killers than Nitzah. Nitzah didn't want to hurt anyone and held the Revolutionary Army in contempt. Rosa and Andy proved themselves to be excellent soldiers. They were stealthy as cats, and as patient and deadly. Rosa had been working as a barista in the Little Cafe in Holyoke where businessmen and bohemians would gather. I would learn much later that Rosa was also a prostitute who sold herself on the side to try to save enough money to buy her own house; she hated paying rent. Andy worked as a farm hand. Even Andy, with his respectable job, had all sorts of stick and poke tattoos and wore his hair in that funny asymmetrical queer haircut. He was one of the best at commanding in the heat of battle. With just looks and gestures he could get men to act in perfect concert to surprise and destroy the enemy. Andy could see into the designs of his enemies, and utterly out-maneuver and rout them.

Before the fighting had broken out, I was an adjunct Professor of Physics at the University of Massachusetts and did small engine repair as a hobby and little side hustle. After most of the University was shut down during the civil war, I was out of the job. In the ill-starred Battle of St. Paul, I was wounded and sent home. The government wasn't able to pay me what it had promised, and I had to scramble to put my understanding of physics into mechanics to keep my kids from starving. Fifteen years later, when the Revolutionary Army came around, it was my best option. They were able to pay in good silver, and my salary kept food on the table back home. Later, I'd return to the campus and took great pleasure in watching all thirty stories of the WEB DuBois Library burn to the ground.

I've never been skilled as a military strategist, and I relied on better minds to help me in making tactical and strategic decisions. My skill is getting others to follow me and to even enjoy walking the path that I beat.

Andy

We had a hopeless and agonizing love triangle. Like most all love triangles, there were winners and losers. Nitzah and I won at Rosa's expense. When I first met them, after my family moved to the Pioneer Valley, they were luminous with their love. Young love has a certain shallowness; but it is also illuminating like a flame cutting into the darkness. There is something revelatory about the unfolding of young love. When we first met we all immediately became friends. Nitzah was beautiful to me, otherworldly. She was an herbalist and was so steady in her practice. On top of that, we shared some interests in literature. We both had to fight to find the time to read books, and it was a revelation to discuss literature with someone else possessed by the same sort of passion. Rosa was a fierce and dangerous woman who wordlessly commanded respect. She worked at Holyoke's most popular cafe and prostituted herself on the side to save money for a house, I think. When the fighting hit she lost her savings and then she joined the Revolutionary Army. Of course, after we won she would have been able to get her house, but she died of dysentery a few weeks before the official peace settlement.

We all lived within a few miles of each other in South Hadley, across the river from Holyoke. We had bicycles and there were more bicycles on the roads than cars except the big pickups so angrily driven by the men who would start the Revolution. Anger was something of a fashion in those days; the soldiers would compete with stories of their grave insults, but I stayed aloof. Anger always struck me as a wasteful emotion to indulge in, especially when there are so many more pleasant ones.

Nitzah and Rosa shared a bed in a tiny room in a collective house in South Hadley. Rosa earned the money to pay rent and Nitzah grew food and made trades and brought home a small income from her herbal practice. They seemed to greatly enjoy their domestic routine. At least, before I came and ruined everything.

Since we shared interests and there weren't a lot of people our age around we began spending a lot of time together. I'd bike the four miles to visit them and then the four miles back to work on the farm early the next morning.

On one special day I came over and then it began raining. It must have been a Saturday because I don't think I had work the day after. Rosa took out a bottle of rum and we laughed and took shots and somehow all three of us fell into bed. Without the littlest thought, we all made love that night. Equally without thought, Nitzah and I choose each other to the exclusion of Rosa that night. We never had a threesome again, and Nitzah told me sometime after that night that she realized how much more she desired men than women. Nitzah was the first transwoman I was in a relationship with but not the last. On my part, I desired Nitzah more than Rosa. It is odd, I wouldn't have thought that to be how things would turn out, but as already mentioned, very little thought was involved. We very simply fell in love and equally simply broke Rosa's heart like dropping a fresh cartoon of eggs.

Rose and I shared something that Nitzah and I never did; we shared our mutual hatred for each other. This helped us to become a highly effective military unit after the Revolution broke out. Our hate kept us in form; it sharpened our resolve and connected us psychically like lovers, but without any of the distracting romantic sentimentality.

When the revolutionary force first swept through, burning the giant library at U-Mass, sacking Mount Holyoke and murdering anyone who stood in its way as "degenerates," I hated them. I hated how they were killing clueless rich kids "for the children," and their hang ups about purity. Indeed, had there been an organized counter-revolutionary force I would have joined it. Instead, I became one of their best tactical commanders.

Nitzah

Andy and I were making love right when the Revolutionary Army kicked down our bedroom door. Or Rosa's door, rather; she was sleeping on the common couch downstairs. I felt offended that these teenage boys were pointing rifles at me and my boyfriend, and that they interrupted us in the middle of our love. What outrage! Luckily, Andy was a very smooth talker with a silver tongue. He had a natural genius for diplomacy, and with a few words he managed to have us dress, grabbed some kava tincture and poured himself a shot. Soon we were all drinking kava and then we moved onto the lemon balm, hawthorn, ghost pipe and California poppy. We woke with the soldiers three days later with a splitting headache. Rosa was there with us on the floor too. We asked if we could enlist and the boys liked the idea so I gathered my vulnerary herbs and bandages and we went marching out into the early summer morning.

Andy never failed to impress me, even when he impressed me with his capacity for evil. During a massacre he had the same calculating coldness as when he talked us into joining the army, which was really the best bet for our survival at the time.

We three marched to headquarters with the young soldiers not as captives but as equals, perhaps even a bit superior. Indeed, when the Sergeant Major saw us and sized us up, he immediately promoted us so that we wouldn't have to take orders from our captors ever again.

CHAPTER 3: WAITING

Sergeant Major

Before the Battle of Granby, we had been in contact with a man on the inside, the Granby chief of police who communicated to us by radio. He had been manufacturing methamphetamine, which we hoped to use in our military maneuvers. Before we took Granby, he was executed by decision of the Town Council. He had mentioned that he was under investigation for his illegal drug manufacturing and he also had indicated that some people had caught whiff that he was sympathetic to the Revolution. Perhaps that is in part why they killed him. There was no way to tell after Granby had been reduced to smoldering rubble. I had sincerely liked the man; he had a sense of humor. He was an opportunist like myself rather than a true believer. I liked him; even in those dark days he could get me to chuckle over our scratchy radio conversations.

Granby had much of the prime farmland we needed to control in order to feed our troops. We sent out a scout to settle our terms of negotiation; we would offer protection, I would personally promise that our Soldiers wouldn't cause any undue harm unpunished, and we would ask for food hoards, but would leave more than enough to last till the kitchen gardens were producing again in the spring. If people didn't relinquish their property to us, we would then be justified in taking it from them by force.

This was the standard sort of surrender we had negotiated time and time again. This was a simple procedure. Often times we were even able to negotiate better taxes than the United States government. More often than not, we only needed our heavy artillery as a set piece to convince people it would be a really bad idea to try to resist.

The people of Granby were definitely extra stupid that day or maybe just principled. Maybe they didn't like that we wished to make them our vassals. Maybe they were, as usual, drunk by noon. What we do know is that we sent three horsemen in, one after the other, with white flags and our generous terms of surrender, and one after the other they were shot dead.

Something deep and evil was unleashed in the Revolutionary Army. To this day I don't know who gave orders to begin the bombardment. Nonetheless, once it began I didn't stop it. For twelve hours we rained fire bombs on top of Granby. Most all the houses were made of wood, and within twenty-four hours at least eight-five percent of the buildings were smoking rubble. We used drones and helicopters to seek out people hiding in the forest. The Chinese had excellent infrared vision cameras we used to find the potential rebels and kill them dead.

After three terrible days we had approximately fifty casualties. They lost two thousand. Finally, after a week there was a formal surrender. This time we offered no terms. We disarmed the entire town. We forced the men to gather the bodies of the slain in wheelbarrows and dump them in a great hole we had dug with large machines. This took three days. Many of these men sickened from handling so many corpses. When the bodies were all in the hole we lined the men up on the edge of the hole and sprayed them with bullets. Then we used great diesel machines to cover them with dirt.

The Revolutionary Army wintered in Granby. We ate mostly horse meat. I am ashamed that my troops took so many vulgar liberties with the women and children. Granby became known as the degenerate town and its residents were viewed as subhuman. The residents were used as slave labor to salvage metal out of their destroyed liquor stores and work in a munitions factory building our arms. The Chinese were happy to offer their technical savvy in making the munitions factory. Of course, after we won, the factory was torn down and the Chinese revealed their hand, and an elegant long con it was, to be our masters. And they won; we may have crushed the old United States, but China controlled both the boats and the satellites and the future belonged to them.

So they became our masters. I was given a large land grant to operate a pig farm. A few years later I died a broken man, deeply shamed at the betrayal I had helped set into motion.

Rosa

Why do you wake me? I am sleepy, my soul is ready to claim me and my debts are repaid. Why do you call me?

There are few things to say. While I was alive I was strong and formidable and was always accepted as one of the boys and also one of the girls. This was the same with the Revolutionary army. In a reckless love affair my heart was broken and I died before I could recover, but now that all seems so long ago and so trivial.

I participated in the battle of Granby, the deadliest battle of the entire Revolution. There I shot no less than forty-five men dead. Some of these deaths haunt me still, some do not.

The thing that really disturbs my rest, is a memory I have after the Battle of Granby. We were filled with the diabolical force of victory. We were split into small platoons to subdue the entire town of Granby, all of the little homesteads scattered here and there. Andy, Nitzah, and I were in the same platoon. There were others, too. We found a farmhouse. Nitzah still didn't have a gun, and had just a few days to live.

We came upon the farmhouse and there were a few dogs outside that barked and acted as if they would bite us. As they approached we shot them with high powered calibers and they burst into little red clouds as we laughed.

We kicked down the door and the husband tried to surrender. He was shot. His wife, an unusually beautiful woman, was greedily raped by the soldiers. Andy somehow stopped the madness. He kicked her and her two children out, and got Nitzah to walk them somewhere else. No one was really commanding, instead we followed the same diabolic impulse.

That entire winter the devil walked with us. It became worse after Nitzah died. During that winter I developed dysentery. The Sergeant Major was able to save me for a time with a formula Nitzah had taught him: black walnut hull, blackberry root and a pinch of cayenne. I was weakened and died in a high fever just around the spring equinox.

Now my ghost is old and at peace. I am but a murmur and soon my soul shall claim me.

Nitzah

After I stumbled into the farmhouse and saw the poor woman bleeding from her legs, her husband's brains all over the dining room table and soldiers' feces in the closets, I was taken over by a terrible desire to kill every last revolutionary fighter. Andy had the presence of mind to have me take the poor stunned woman and her children to another farmhouse, though she took me to the barn instead, snarling, "I'm not showing you where our neighbors live." I brought out her linens and blankets so she and her children wouldn't die of exposure during the night. That being done, and with the sun setting, I smoked all of my hashish and wandered down to a little stream. In my jacket pocket I kept a two-ounce tincture bottle of poison hemlock root. Sitting by the river by dry iris leaves, I drank all of the foul liquid in one swallow. Darkness ringed my vision and soon I was standing by my body, dead but not released.

Andy

After the war I settled down to an estate that grew apples for the hard cider that had become fashionable in China. My ma had shared her interest in permaculture with me, and I set out to make the most efficient food production systems. My apples produced some of the best hard cider in all of the Republic of New England. Later, I learned that my product was considered very highly by Chinese connoisseurs. My cider even became something of a status symbol among the entrepreneurial classes in China.

The woman who was raped in the farmhouse was named Linda. Through a long set of improbable circumstances, she became my mistress after the war, and I was able to protect her and her charming children from the excesses of the revolution.

While it was never said out loud, I considered Linda to be my wife and I treated her children as if they were my own. With time we developed real affection and love. We were a family, and the degree to which we were a loving family is the degree to which I found peace in our little domestic routines. I cherished the eighteen years we got to spend together in our fragile shared happiness.

Witnessing so much fighting, my heart became not only broken but hard, and I began to be tormented by morbid fantasy. Over time the aches and pains in my heart grew like a vigorous weed and one day my heart heaved and refused to work anymore. I slumped over my desk, dead.

Unfortunately for my wife and children, they were unofficial and thus met an unpleasant fate after I died, being contracted to mine resources out of some of the dead cities. I was not able to die peacefully and so I restless walk the land in death seeking the peace that eluded me during life.

Nitzah

The other ghosts are not aware that they are waiting. They think they are searching; they think that they are going to find the answer of the riddles of their lives. That isn't a correct way to look at things. I know that I am simply waiting. I know that I am a little fragment that my soul left to be healed at some future point. My soul doesn't know everything, and she doesn't know how to incorporate my experiences, yet.

This is the major problem with suicide. Afterwards, the soul is bewildered and then you have to wait. After taking your life you must endure decades of waiting. Not even other ghosts can alleviate this tedium. Ghosts are horrible conversational partners. They do not listen, they just want to go on and on for weeks about their problems without letting you get a word in edgewise. Maybe these monologues help relieve the boredom of waiting. They don't seem to change much besides that though.

Because I suffered so deeply and ended my life in such suffering, my suffering is deeper than most other ghosts. So my consciousness is relatively more expansive than that of fellow phantoms. I am more self-aware, at least enough to know that I am a ghost and that I am waiting.

What I've learned in this waiting is that the soul is both a subject and an object;

the soul gets stuck in space and time. We are little more than the habits we inhabit and the momentum of choices carried from life to life.

When I was fifteen I tried to become a woman through a crude surgical process, and my soul told me, in good humor I might add, that a future incarnation will have to carry my decision as a deformity. I and I alone am responsible for both what I have done and what has happened to me. Whenever I talk with my soul she is unfailingly in good humor and indeed whenever we have the pleasure of conversing it brightens my week.

It is easy to be hard on myself while I wait, but I must be fair; I made good choices along with my many bad ones. A dream at twelve convinced me to never touch alcohol or opium, and then I also taught Oliver, that roughneck orphan, the mysteries of herbalism for the seven years before the fighting broke out. I never did learn what happened to Oliver, but I like to imagine that he lived longer than I did and was able to maintain his decency. I could have been much crueler to other people and at many points I showed admirable restraint and mercy. But in my interminable solitude I see that I was wrong to kill myself; it was a stupid mistake.

You can't lie to yourself when you only have yourself to talk to for hundreds of years. Eventually you are forced to admit checkmate to yourself, because it is you and only you waiting together. All of the phantoms and desires and thoughts and feelings separate and when they talk it is revealed that there is only you; you are parts of you.

I've spent such a long time waiting here that I even had to stop being jaded and cynical. Now I am innocent as a child, but still I am responsible and still I wait.

CHAPTER 4: ALGUNAS NOTAS

Luna Hueca

Over the next several months Girasol and I worked to arrange the stories of the ghosts. After much debate and discussion, we settled on the current arrangement of the narrative, both the portions we remembered personally and those Girasol caught in his telarañas. It was what felt most natural to me, and Girasol grudgingly conceded that it was good, or at least good enough. Neither of us still feels haunted by our prior incarnation.

With great joy we carried the sheet music and recorders from the mountains. Over the next few years I was able to teach five children and two adults to sight read music and play most of the concertos. In a few weeks I intend to buy a cello from the great workshops in old Appalachia, and to perform some of Vivaldi's concertos with other musicians for the town.

Before he died, Girasol made sure to train eight apprentices in his mysteries. He told me with much pride that several of his brighter students were threatening to surpass him in herb craft, but sadly no one could touch his telaraña weaving abilities. Perhaps with fewer ghosts the art of the Eight Strings will eventually be forgotten. When he died serenely two years ago I believe that he henceforth found freedom, or perhaps rather his soul did. I miss him, but he comes into my dreams from time to time and when he does he gently blesses me.

Perhaps then all there is to say is that my life has been entirely fair, that I have earned all of my experiences and have more to earn I am sure in my next incarnation. I remember now something that Listo used to say during our lessons: "Your life is the truth that you seek."

And now I may be the last alive of the old village of La Vezita. This is the end of this manuscript. I don't know what to do with it, but it is something so alive and sacred to me that I wish with all my breath that it may have a life of its own.

Archivist's Note

We are grateful to our great Queen and generous benefactress Hojas Verdes. May she reign in peace for the next century!

A shepherd seeking a lost lamb stumbled upon this very unusual manuscript. While searching, he happened upon a strange library in a mountain cave in the Connecticut River Valley, several miles out of the great city of Holyoke. The cave appears to be of human construction, with excellent design features that help control humidity to levels that are ideal for preserving hemp paper and string.

The shepherd reported his find to the proper authorities in Holyoke, who then uncovered a chest, which contained some of the oldest Vivaldi and Telemann sheet music that we have yet to discover, although we've discovered older and more complete Bach works outside of old Brattleboro.

On the walls were many rough-hewn shelves holding masses of tied string. The string appears to be tied in distinct patterns that are used as a mnemonic device, as is referenced many times in the text. We have lost the key to the system, but of course we teach a similar, although simplified, technique at all public schools. Perhaps it is not too bold to say that our focus on mnemonics originates in visually beautiful string tying techniques evident in these caves. We hung the strings in a museum of history, until we received complaints from the visitors pleading with us to take them down out of respect to the ghosts which had begun to menace their dreams.

This manuscript, the only complete one that we have yet to find, helps us to put some of the attitudes and practices of the tumultuous late medieval period into context, and helps to clarify feelings around the legacy of the ancient world.

It is interesting to wonder how much the author was talking about ghosts or the pernicious effects of the ancient pollution which poisoned many urban areas. Science had been persecuted for several centuries before the Renaissance of the last century, and so people tended towards mystical explanations during this period rather than analyze phenomena rationally.

Another interesting point of this manuscript is that it anticipates many of the scientific discoveries we have made concerning the soul and its incarnations and ghosts, which is why I have decided to publish this odd and fragmentary book for the scholars that utilize this university library. I have written extensively on childhood recollections of past lives, ghosts and demons, and when I was made aware of this text by a colleague I found it frankly uncanny how much it bears out with the prevailing theories.

We believe that this manuscript was copied at least two times. Through careful analysis, the paper reveals itself to be about three hundred years old. In the same cave there is an older copy that is much decayed with age, about four hundred years old. This is probably the original. The newer, more complete copy dates to around the time of The Great Consolidation, when rediscovered military technology allowed Ohio to gain control of the eastern third of North America, fulfilling the ancient legend of Death's Promise. Of course this is the time that the seeds of our own civilization began to sprout and grow.

We hope that the reader can forgive the odd mysticisms and religious sensibility and has appreciated this unique perspective into a long forgotten age.

CODA

The Prospect of a New Gothic Age in the United States

by Karl North

HUMAN SOCIETY FACES AN UNPRECEDENTED, irreparable shift away from industrial civilization that ultimately will prove catastrophic for most people. A large part of the global population has a cultural heritage that derives from the age of monotheisms that began about two millennia ago. This heritage persists despite strong secularization trends that began in recent centuries with the age of science, industrialization, rationality and progress. This cultural heritage in all three major monotheisms—Judaism, Islam and Christianity—shapes how people react to times of great change, insecurity and extended crisis such as the one humanity faces today.

This pattern of response to long emergencies consists of a constellation of elements that first appeared in the formative period of these religions because the very emergence of monotheism was a reaction to extremely unsettled conditions of those times. The rise of the monotheisms served a need for new social and belief structures to address the inability of the ageing Roman empire and the existing pantheistic religious cultures to cope with the chaotic warring city state polities of the late classical age.

The characteristic response of the monotheisms is to create a community of the faithful that closes ranks in a totalitarian social order that depicts human life as threatened on all sides with damnation but open to salvation. This form of society pursues violent crusades against external infidels and internal heretics, carries out harsh punishments for sinners, and holds out an apocalyptic vision of salvation as a last resort.

My goal here is to explore the potential for this type of response to deindustrialization to occur in the United States, given our distinctive cultural heritage that has been heavily influenced by the Protestant Reformation of Christianity. I will first describe the Gothic age and the Reformation as the last major incarnation in Christian culture of the characteristic response in monotheisms to long periods of social insecurity and crisis. Then I will draw attention to historical and current developments in US society that suggest the likelihood of a new Gothic age in this country. Awareness of this probable future will hopefully help us think of ways to navigate it.

THE GOTHIC AGE

Oswald Spengler's *The Decline of the West* is an extremely detailed history of the evolution of society through three great ages of religious culture. His treatment has given me a new appreciation of the violent and scary periods in the age of monotheisms that replaced the age of classical pantheism of gods in most parts of the Western world. Recognized as Gothic Christianity in Europe, this early development in the age of monotheisms had counterparts with similar characteristics in early Islam and Judaism as well. Its manifestation in Islam, for instance, is the violent crusading zeal of its early period, preserved today by the Saudi medieval monarchy as Wahhabism, whose jihadi militants are used by the Western powers as proxies in the attempt to destabilize and destroy regimes that show resistance to imperial control in the Middle East. In Judaism the best parallel today to Gothic Christianity is the militantly expansionist, openly racist theocratic state of Israel and its Zionist supporters, both Jewish and Christian fundamentalist, in the United States and Europe. In both Judaism and Islam, I would identify these responses as current reactions to crisis that are typical of all societies that have the monotheistic heritage described above. When not in periods of crisis or instability, religious practices in these societies take more moderate forms.

Gothic Christianity grew out of the difficult period following the collapse of the Roman Empire in Europe. The age was punctuated with repeated invasions, marauding warlords, and recurrent epidemics of bubonic plague that appeared in the unsanitary town life that revived toward the end of the period. The Church became the main creator of social order. As a result, in Gothic times humans perceived life as a frightful slippery slope with handholds upward toward the light and salvation offered by the church, but also filled with satanic beings that constantly tormented and tempted them down toward damnation. It was a time of crusades against the infidel and the extermination of presumed heretics. Inside the community of the faithful the grip of the church was totalitarian; in theory no aspect of life escaped its demand of total obedience. Outside that community was the void, which offered nothing of value. In Gothic culture, history would eventually end with the violent triage of the apocalypse, which would save only those who had remained within the community of the faithful.

The tumult of the Protestant Reformation provoked Gothic society to further extremes, the 17th century seeing a million witches burned at the stake. Here is

Spengler on the effect of the Reformation:

> The Reformation abolished the whole bright and consoling side of the Gothic myth—the cult of Mary, the venerations of the saints, the relics, the pilgrimages, the mass. But the myth of devil-dom and witchcraft remained, for it was the embodiment and cause of the inner torture, and now that torture at last rose to its supreme horror. Baptism was, for Luther at least, an exorcism, the veritable sacrament of devil-banning. There grew up a large, purely Protestant literature about the Devil. Out of the Gothic wealth of colour, there remained black. . . . [I]t is a true Myth that inheres in the firm belief in dwarfs, bogies, nixies, house-sprites and sweeping clouds of the disembodied and a true Cult that is seen in the rites, offerings, and conjurings that are still practiced with a pious awe.

Here is an illustration typical of the plight of a politically incorrect Puritan in Reformation Europe and early colonial North America as well:

The Europeans eventually exiled many of the most extremist sects of the Reformation Goths to the colonies across the Atlantic that became the United States of America, where many elements of Protestant Gothic culture have survived in the puritanism that spread out of New England and in the apocalyptic rapturism of the born-again Christians who today are alleged to number nearly half of the US population. In secularized Europe, where magnificent cathedrals stand empty except for summer tourists, people shook their heads in amusement at the election of our first born-again Christian president, Jimmy Carter. How quaint, they thought! When the second one appeared (like a burning Bush?), Europeans began to wonder if Yankee society and culture ever was going to emerge from infancy. In Europe, All Saints Day is now mainly an occasion to visit the cemetery and remember the dead. Only in America has it become full-blooded Gothic, a scary day of satanically grinning jack-o-lanterns, witches riding on broomsticks, and ghosts of the dead who arise to torment the living. Despite the tongue-in-cheek children's entertainment aspect, the event is only a step away from the real thing.

Gothic Christianity was a gradual response to the long period of unstable conditions in Europe that replaced the relative calm of the Pax Romana: economic insecurity in shifting, poorly reconstituted medieval polities, recurrent plagues that invaded the growing but unsanitary cities of the High Middle Age, weather-related famines like the Little Ice Age, all took their toll. The long emergency of increasing energy and resource scarcity and the ensuing degrowth is likely to bring about similar conditions.

Indicators of a New Gothic Age in the United States of America

As Gothic culture in its Protestant form survives better in the United States than in most Western societies, here I will point to some signs I see today that surviving Gothic remnants in this country may become the basis of a cultural response to the experiences of the age of degrowth that we are entering. Early warnings of a possible new age of Goths in the United States include the following:

1. The increasing penetration of US federal and state governments by proponents of a totalitarian Christian state. The current president, while showing little evidence of Christian faith, has nevertheless populated top levels of his administration with militant Gothic Christians to retain the loyalty of groups of similar faith that populate his electoral base. The number of militant Christians in Congress continues to increase. The vice president in the Trump administration exemplifies fanatical Gothic Christianity.

2. Not to be outdone, the liberal identity politics movement, wielding a hysterical and increasingly rigid notion of political correctness (PC), is fielding its own militant totalitarians in a crackdown on all speech that invades "safe spaces," starting in academia where speakers have been chased off campus and faculty careers have been destroyed for saying the wrong word. The government and its media and internet servants are using these liberal betrayals of free speech as an opportunity to

increasingly curtail and ban speech that dissents from any part of the ruling class narrative. Laws dating from the Bush and Obama administrations permit prosecution of "treasonous" dissenters as terrorist suspects. Official lists of suspects exist. A new version of the McCarthyite witch hunt culture of the hysterically anti-communist 1950s is forming, itself patterned on the witch hunt culture of colonial New England, Gothic to the core of its joyless purity.

3. For now, the ruling oligarchy is happy to encourage both the above trends, but they could easily get out of control, as has happened with its use of Islamic jihadi militias as proxies in its Middle East wars. Both increasingly totalitarian movements are displaying the propensity to indulge in crusades against heretics. Ruling elites may be losing the ability to use the crusader element in US Gothic culture to retain support for foreign wars, so they are turning it inward to energize internecine conflicts that divert attention from more fundamental problems of society. The no-holds-barred politics of the so-called alt-right supremacists, the militant Gothic Christians, the identity politics PC liberals and the antifa alt-left are all taking on rudiments of Gothic crusader culture, branding their opponents as infidels or even the Anti-Christ (the modern favored equivalent being Hitler) and labeling internal dissent as heresy.

Late European Gothic culture included the Romantic reaction against the age of hell-bent progress, science and the machine—a reaction embodied in North American sects like the Amish and Hutterites. In contrast, a prospective Gothic revival today would occur in a society generally addicted to the religion of progress, so it would likely take novel forms to incorporate this difference. One such twist is the growing habit of hostile groups in the United States to accuse each other of failing to save the American Way of Life, with each entertaining radically different interpretations of what that means. For Spengler, the age of progress that has progressively replaced the age of monotheisms is a Faustian deal with the devil that therefore contains its own abundant share of bogies, hobgoblins, gremlins and inconvenient consequences, more than enough to cause the modern system to self-destruct.

Spengler says it's important to see the history of Gothic culture in its full intensity, because moderns have tried to forget or suppress its exotic horrors as too impossibly primitive to ever have happened to our "enlightened" species. But its vestiges, at least in US culture, suggest a more enduring element that can reappear in some guise under historical conditions of sufficient stress.

Don't miss a single issue of Into the Ruins

Made in the USA
Middletown, DE
26 July 2019